# STERLING FIERCE AND THE LOST DRAGONS

# STERLING FIERCE AND THE LOST DRAGONS

## STERLING FIERCE
### BOOK ONE

## LORI TCHEN

WISE WOLF
BOOKS

WISE WOLF BOOKS
An Imprint of Wolfpack Publishing
wisewolfbooks.com
701 S. Howard Ave. 106-324, Tampa, FL 33609

Cover design by Wise Wolf Books

Paperback ISBN 978-1-957548-86-9
eBook ISBN 978-1-957548-85-2
LCCN 2023951267

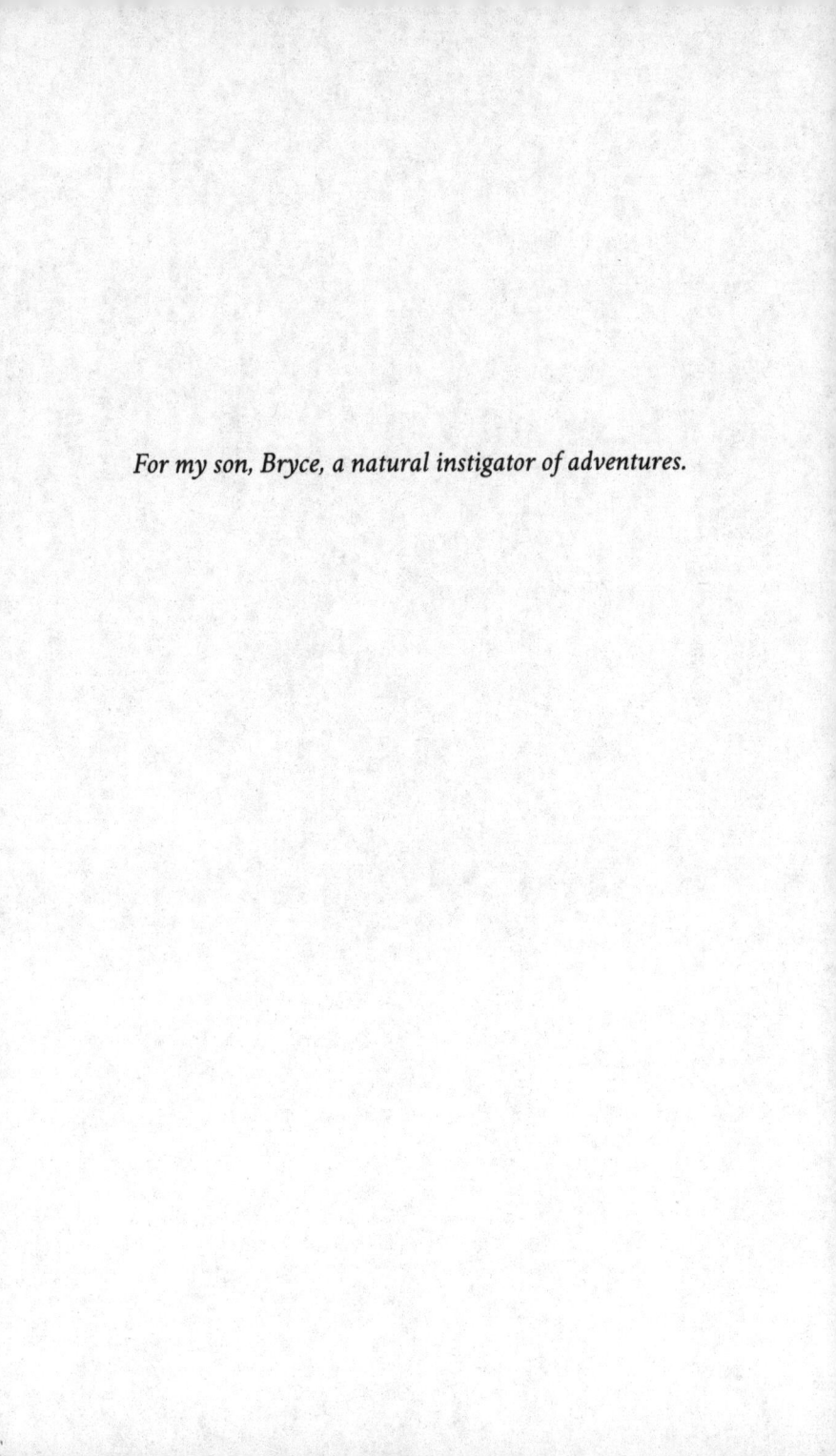

*For my son, Bryce, a natural instigator of adventures.*

# STERLING FIERCE AND THE LOST DRAGONS

# CHAPTER ONE
# A NEBULOUS QUEST BEGINS

S terling Fierce had journeyed all the way from the village of Bren for one purpose—to go inside this cave. The cave without a name. He peered inside the pitch-black hole until his eyes and ears adjusted as they did on night hunts. As a born witch hunter, his senses were acutely sensitive when they needed to be, and he had been honing his hunting skills for the past year. The drip-splash of moisture onto rock became as loud as choppy waves against a worn-out boat, and a tall, shadowy figure wearing a pointed wizard's cap came into view.

*And here's to another successful hunt—we've got one isolated wizard in the middle of a hidden island,* Sterling thought. Too bad tracking him wasn't the hard part. He swallowed. *I really hope he doesn't turn me into a toad or worse.*

Sterling was no stranger to the magic world, but he'd never met a wizard before. He was about to meet the most famous potion wizard in Everen and wasn't entirely sure what to expect. Equally unknown was how the wizard would react to an unwelcome guest— or in this case, an average-looking boy of fourteen with messy, brown shoulder-length hair and a slender build covered in hand-me-down trousers and a tattered blue cape. But at a closer look, Sterling's stormy gray eyes were clear and piercing—with pupils like those of the wild creatures he hunted. He was anything but average.

"I promise, Sterling, you will find this to be a most fascinating journey. Some long-awaited answers will come to you along the way," the Alin had said, before sending the young witch hunter on his quest south. The village elder had been evasive when Sterling had asked for more details, but Sterling had agreed to travel beyond the Sea of Grunne to an isle so remote it wouldn't be found on any maps.

Surrounded by gray-sand beaches and with no other islands in sight, it was easy for Sterling to forget the rest of Everen. The sandy shores carved a shallow ring around the mainland that gave way to a grand circle of trees so tall, they bent inward, interlocking their branches and hiding the center of the island completely.

Alins had ancient blood. They were healers and seers who could read the destinies of others. Tomorak, the Alin in Sterling's home village of Bren, was centuries old, likely to live centuries more. Like most Alins, he watched over the villagers, mostly farmers, fishermen, some hunters, and one esteemed mapmaker, Sterling's Uncle Roag.

The more Tomorak's words rattled in his mind, the more of a riddle this quest became. Answers— what answers could he mean? Sterling had been happy in Bren, farming his father's pecan trees...*Oh stardust, even I know that's a lie. I want—need—an adventure, to discover something new. Maybe there's something out here in the wild—something that needs to be discovered too.*

Being a witch hunter meant that even at fourteen years old, Sterling had abilities more remarkable than most men. He could track animals better than an expert hunter and had the strength of several burly men. But his most valuable skill was tracking and destroying witches—something he'd had to do a couple of times since his powers revealed themselves. He hadn't even meant to find the first witch he'd destroyed. She had found him. The connection between witches and witch hunters wasn't fully understood, and Sterling was forced to discover his abilities alone. He was the only living witch hunter in Everen now that his father, Sir Rider Fierce, was dead.

His shoulders twitched at the thought of the witches he'd faced, one of whom was responsible for the diseased, bewitched bear that had killed his father. It had been only a year since the bear took his father's life, but it felt like an eternity to Sterling.

There were no magic creatures viler than witches. However, Fire Dragons were a close second from what he'd seen of them in the Eastlands. He hoped wizards were nothing like any of them. He figured the wizard had sensed his arrival the second he and his horse touched the island's sandy shores, probably before then. Whether that was good or bad, he would soon find out.

*You never know about the magic kind*, villagers from Bren always warned.

After a few deep breaths, he pushed aside a childhood rhyme about a wizard turning a boy into a toad and stepped inside for a better look.

Taking full advantage of his enhanced hunter's vision, Sterling studied the potion wizard as the man darted to and fro inside the cave. A purple glow highlighted the outline of a wizard's kitchen, set atop a flat layer of rock. One large cauldron sat at its center, surrounded by potion bottles and tubes and what looked like measuring tools.

So far, the wizard hadn't acknowledged the young witch hunter breaching the entrance of his well-hidden lair. Boulders as gigantic as one-story huts camouflaged the cave's opening, nestled within a dense forest backdrop. Behind the cave, everything blurred with green and mud-brown leaves tall enough to block the ocean-hugging shoreline. It was a strange island—no way to see in, no way to see out.

Sterling's senses were on high alert, and soon the damp cave air felt like lead in his lungs. He brushed his finger against his upper lip, which had recently started growing a downy mustache, although it would be years before his beard rivaled that of his uncle. He shivered and climbed outside. Instead of fresh forest leaves, the ocean humidity clogged his nose with salty air and hints of decayed seaweed.

*This wizard picked the most desolate island for his work for a reason. He doesn't want to be found and certainly not interrupted. I'll have to go down there and be a bother—but not yet,* Sterling figured, tightening the leather binding around his dagger.

# CHAPTER TWO
## TANGLEWOODS

S terling took a deep breath as he left the cave. There had been no other travelers in his path beyond the southernmost tip of Everen's mainland, which was a relief. Everen was vast, and much of it was uninhabitable for humans unless venomous swamp flies or Sand Dragons were your preferred neighbors. This island was one of many that made up the Isles of Grunne. It was said to be unpopulated. So far, it had been, except for the occasional flock of blackbirds that had been spooked by Sterling's horse, Banefield. Sterling also spotted one cat-sized lizard, tattooed with territory battle scars, who seemed disinterested in him or anything else.

*Maybe he's retired from fighting—the poor guy looks plain ol' tired.*

Unlike the scarred lizard, Sterling wasn't tired. A strong desire ran through him, more than anything, to honor his Fierce family name and prove he deserved to stay in his village. His home, Bren, was an old farmer's town with rich soil for growing all sorts of vegetables and fruit (pocket berries were his favorite...pocket berry pies sounded delightful right now). It was situated near the Windly Stream, a sizable split of the Great River and a plentiful source of fish. Enormous golden wheat fields on both edges of the village shone in the wind, and soft-sloped hills popped up like a protective border slowly transitioning to the thick pines of Bear Woods. It was his only home, and if he didn't complete Tomorak's quests, returning to Bren wouldn't be an option. All villagers were expected to contribute to the village's well-being. Without his father around to perform big game hunts and haul in enough meat to last a whole winter, there was considerable pressure on Sterling to earn his land.

Before mustering up the nerve to step back inside the cave, he skipped away from the looming boulders and down a steep grassy decline. He spread his cape out flat against the lush ground and slid downhill. The wind pressed against his face, and he smiled with glee as he picked up speed. Near the bottom of the hill, the soft padding beneath him transformed abruptly into knotted tree roots jutting out of mud. He tumbled forward, landing on a mess of tree roots braided in and around one another.

*This isn't good. Twisted, tangled tree roots—just like in father's stories. But these can't be tanglewood trees, can they?*

"Ancient deadly snakes live in the hollow roots of tanglewood trees. Their bite is so potent, a single drop would kill a grown man in seconds," Sterling said, repeating what his father would have spouted out. "In the darkness of their wooden canals, the snakes evolved glowing eyes to light their way, or so the stories tell." The hairs on the back of Sterling's arms stood straight up when he imagined what the snakes might look like.

*Tanglewood serpents don't exist—just another one of Father's stories*, he reassured himself, brushing his upper lip again. He stepped cautiously over the wooden braids and tried not to think about the possibility of bubble-eyed serpents writhing inches below. He'd had enough run-ins with creepy creatures to last him a lifetime and decided he'd rather not add tanglewood serpents to the list.

Sir Rider Fierce had raised him to be watchful of the world around him, and Sterling's bedtime stories had never been without witches, giants, fairies, or other magical creatures. His father's stories were an extension of his spirit, weaving together and guiding Sterling like an invisible thread. But sometimes it was hard to know which stories were just stories and which were not. Despite the obvious safety risks, lately, he'd grown more curious about the oddities throughout Everen—part of him yearned to investigate and discover more.

Clearing a long stretch of tanglewoods, he lunged beneath a shower of oval-shaped leaves and dangling shelled nuts that clunked together like wooden wind chimes. It smelled like his tree farm when the pecans were ripe, but the ground was marshy and not at all like the firm soil back in Bren. He trudged ahead, but his boots sank into the wet ground. Plucking his legs out of the mud (and keeping his boots on) proved more difficult with each step. Sweat bled through his flimsy cotton shirt and poured from his bushy brown hair.

This island was a handful, even for him. He smacked away a flurry of hanging branches and dodged more tanglewood roots.

*More of these serpent trees? Maybe there are hundreds of creepy glowing eyes slithering inside just waiting to crawl out of a hole somewhere. Or maybe they don't exist at all.*

With some clumsy luck and instinctual sense of direction, he finally made his way to a clearing he recognized.

Banefield, his trusted horse, snuggled beneath drooping tree branches and grazed on leaves. The leaves smelled strangely sweet, like boiling sugar mixed with horse sweat. Banefield's shiny tail swished from side to side in a relaxed way, and green-tinted slobber slung happily from his nibbling jaw. His horseshoes glowed pale blue with magic that allowed him to gallop on water. This is how Sterling had traveled across the Sea of Grunne.

"I won't be long, Banefield. I just have to talk to this wizard for the Alin—it's about something important, but no idea what. Then we go home, buddy," Sterling said, half believing the words that fell out of his mouth.

Banefield swiped his tail in silence, flashing glints of silver horsehair that gleamed in the sunlight. His stormy-colored coat shone like it was made of liquid minerals from deep beneath the ground. He released a contented sigh but didn't take his attention off his leafy snack.

*See you soon, my friend.*

Sterling plucked his tattered, midnight-blue cape from the saddle's satchel, fastening it around his neck. He halfheartedly wiped the larger chunks of mud off the half-cloth, half-bear-hide cape. The patches of bear hide weighed him down in a way he found comforting. He'd never been overly concerned about his appearance, but it couldn't hurt to look more put together when he met the potion wizard. He was, after all, representing his Alin and his village, and in a way, his father. He tugged at the edges of the cape. He remembered it reaching a little lower the last time he'd worn it.

Sterling brushed his fingers through the silver mane and scratched Banefield's favorite spot on his neck before departing.

On the way back to the cave, his curiosity about the ancient serpents led him knee-deep in tree roots.

*I'll just be a minute*, he promised himself. *Then, it's right back to the quest.*

He tapped the widest ones with his dagger, but only the sound of hollow knocking answered.

"Nothing lives in here, not even mud beetles. Tanglewood serpents probably don't exist anyway," he said aloud.

Just before returning to the grassy incline that would lead him to the cave, he dragged his metal blade over a heap of wiry tree roots. To his surprise, the wooden bundle returned the telltale clinking sound he'd been searching for but half hoped he wouldn't find.

"What have we here?" Sterling said in a teasing voice.

He lowered himself to ground level, his chest pressed against the damp mud. A thornwing moth fluttered from a clump of nightshade weeds and landed on the tip of his nose.

"Shoo," he said, batting the tiny creature away. But with Sterling's skin in full hunter mode, the prickly leg fur vibrations sparked a terrible itching sensation. He held his nose, but the sneeze burst out anyway. The dagger in his hand jarred loose and sliced across a root. Sterling's wild gray eyes narrowed in as he retrieved the blade.

"The good news is my father was right about these being hollow. This one connects to all the others—it's like a hidden passageway for bugs or—" He paused.

The inside of the root lit up with a ghoulish green glow as two eyes appeared a few inches from the cut root.

"Bad news! The serpents exist!" he exclaimed, pushing away with hunter speed. His heart pounded as he darted toward the cave without a name. He didn't look back, but not out of fear. Instead, he felt a familiar feeling—a connection to his father. A boyish grin beamed across his face as he knew deep down exactly how his father had discovered tanglewood serpents.

Loose dirt sprinkled from his fingers as he adjusted his leather dagger case, a gift from Uncle Roag—a barrel-shaped man whose voice sounded like home. He patted the blade's outline, ensuring it remained neatly pressed into his waist if he needed to fight off cave spiders or an escaped tanglewood serpent. With one arm, then the other, he hoisted his body up the rocky incline until he reached the cave's secret entrance once again.

The wizard's shadow was still busy deep in the cave's center as before. But this time, Sterling was ready.

*It's time to meet this famous potion wizard.*

# CHAPTER THREE

# THE CAVE WITHOUT
# A NAME

Sterling's lungs tightened as he squeezed his body between two enormous boulders. They might as well have been ice giant's toes—they chilled him to his core. Pressing ahead, he weaved in and out of a maze of massive rocks wet from cave drippings and smelling of stone powder and mold. He couldn't see anything except outlines of boulders in the darkness at first, but then the cave widened. Its walls stretched as high as three or four houses stacked on top of each other. The cave floor was one sprawling sheet of uneven rock with puddles where water had eroded holes into it.

Soon, his hunter's vision picked out purple flames flickering across the cave walls. Purple, he knew, was a wizard's color. He was getting closer to the heart of the cave, closer to the potion wizard.

One deep sigh later, he summoned enough courage to descend into the deepest part of the cavern. His head grazed a stalactite, and he ducked, his hunter's instincts helping balance out the unexpected height from his recent growth spurt. He couldn't help but admire the hanging cave formations —some drooped like hardened tears, and others twinkled, dipped in a thousand crystals. Slowly, the coolness of the air put him in better spirits.

*I see why he hides away here. It's beautiful—and quiet. Maybe he won't turn me into a warty toad. Please be a good, normal wizard—if there is such a thing.*

His pupils widened, revealing more than just dark shapes. A massive structure of dangling crystals glittered like a night full of glowing stars. It dripped with sparkling, cube-shaped upside-down piles that dangled from the ceiling like a royal woman's jeweled necklace. A deep violet glow lit up what appeared to be a wizard's kitchen. Its makeshift shelves were stuffed with books—almost as many as his father's library. Most had worn covers stained with ink and magic dust residue. Sterling brushed against wrinkled bits of paper that stuck out of the books as he spider-crawled over stacks of paper.

Then, he reached an array of symbol-covered metal instruments and piles of notebooks (maybe recipe books?) blocking the only walkable path forward.

*This potion wizard is more like a junk collector. How does he work in all this mess?*

He tried to weave around a transparent globe filled with watery liquid. It blinked at him.

*What in Everen?*

Suddenly, his head throbbed. He staggered into a rough towering rock and plunged his hand straight into a heap of sticky silver moss. His fingers stuck in place. He struggled to pull his hand from the rock snot, but its grip held tight. A sharp squeaking sound came from the blinking globe. He didn't want to look at whatever it was doing, but his hand wasn't coming loose.

"Witch hunter! Boy of Bren!" the globe hissed.

He turned, locking eyes with the enchanted sphere as his blood began to run hot, gearing up for attack mode.

"Who are you calling 'boy'?!"

The liquid inside sloshed back and forth violently. Then, something within the globe twitched.

*Smack!*

A fatty eyeball the size of a melon slammed against the glass.

"Yikes, it's rude *and* ugly," Sterling uttered as his body swiveled as far away from the eye as possible.

The eye scanned the cave as Sterling stood as still as he could—he didn't even breathe. But the enormous eyeball wasn't fooled. Its pupil fixated on him and went into a spasm. It flashed electric orange like an angry jack-o'-lantern. Sterling searched for the path ahead, but it was no use. The only way to the wizard led him right next to the ugly, hissing eyeball. To make matters worse, it started to spew goo out of its top and howled like a scalding hot teapot. He tugged his hand with a burst of strength, and it popped free with a splatter of silvery rock glue.

Sterling walked toward the mini volcano-in-a-bowl.

"You can do this. Don't stare. Just don't stare at it."

Slowly, its whispers filled his mind, and he felt a coldness in his stomach that he knew all too well.

*Witches.*

The bulbous eyeball spattered gooey liquid at Sterling as he swept past. But he resisted the urge to weaponize his blood into a bow and arrow.

*Save your energy. It's not worth ruining the quest or offending the wizard. Maybe it's his pet or something.*

Somehow, it whispered even without a mouth. Its words were muddled with angry hisses and gurgles, antagonizing him each step of the way.

"You will pay, hunter boy! Her power lives on in all of us—you cannot defeat us all!"

It had to be a witch's eye—that's why he could understand it. A witch hunter like Sterling was tethered to witches in some way. He always knew when a witch was nearby. No matter which language they spoke (and not that he wanted to), he understood every word. Even the most ancient dialects were easy to decipher. In his experience, witches were all the same. They were full of hatred, jealousy, and greed for power. Witch hunters and witches went back as far as the beginnings of life in Everen. As long as there were witches, there were those with witch-hunting abilities to keep their powerful magic in balance. Life and magic always seemed to seek balance, one of the many lessons his father had taught him.

Sterling strode past, avoiding eye contact and putting as much distance between himself and the witch's eye as possible.

*Such emotional things, witches.*

# CHAPTER FOUR

# THE POTION WIZARD

Returning his focus to the kitchen below, Sterling recalled that this cave was home to at least one other inhabitant, this one just as magical. The potion wizard wore a long, classic robe and had gray-and-white hair down his back. His wizard's cap sat slightly off-center and sparkled in places. He was taller than a human and was busily mixing ingredients inside a giant cauldron with what appeared to be wild, sporadic movements. But Sterling knew wizards always acted with purpose—even if nobody else could appreciate their methods.

The shadow of a pointed cap danced around a cauldron that bore markings from ancient times. The etchings...Sterling had seen some of them before in magic history books. One meant fire, but he couldn't make out the others.

On occasion, Sterling had secretly borrowed books from his Alin's library. If he was to be sent on quests, he needed to learn about Everen and all of its creatures, especially magic ones. He needed to know about horrid things and enchanting things alike. The Alin thought it unwise for a boy to learn too much about magic creatures until he'd matured, but Sterling quietly disagreed.

*Speaking of magic, where did the wizard go?*

Sterling scurried closer, trying not to look like a burglar or to step into cave puddles. Finally, a flat clearing opened before him. It led straight to the wizard's kitchen in the heart of the cave. He took long strides and straightened his back, just like how his father had approached other hunters on important matters.

*Should I say something? Hello or good day, maybe?*

"See here, Barath! It's all about precision with potions. Yes—a dash of this or glob of that'll make the perfect brew. But too much or too little and POOF! Your beard is on fire! Ah yes, no one appreciates such delicate work these days..."

Sterling's eyes darted around the cave's center.

*Wait, who's Barath? There's nobody else here except me.*

The potion wizard frolicked around his kitchen, tossing in ingredients, either unaware or uninterested in his visitor. Then there was a gurgle from the cauldron. A giant bubble rose and burst, puffing colorful powder into the air and splattering different colored liquid. Another bubble rose, this one bigger than the first.

*Pop! Splash!*

Sterling dropped to his stomach. He dodged most of the rainbow explosion, but his face caught a splatter of powdery blue and orange.

"Let's see how it stirs. Delightful! My instincts never fail," the potion wizard exclaimed. "My potion is almost complete!" Enthusiastic words bounced off the cave walls with a booming voice that didn't match the thin elderly man standing next to the giant bubbling brew. "Indeed, I'm both artist and inventor. It's my gift! Barath of Latos—even you can agree!"

*Barath? Is he talking to me—this wizard is crazy!*

Seemingly out of nowhere, another voice creaked, "Behold! He's not an ordinary potion wizard—he's the best potion wizard in all the land. Bah! Just don't blow up this cave with your silly experiment."

A tiny tree shuffled into the wizard's kitchen, muttering to himself.

*Wow! A hybrid species, a meute. I forgot about meutes—they are the loyal companions of wizards. I've never seen one outside of a storybook.*

Barath of Latos stood calmly. His wooden eyebrows rose with suspicion at the spattering potion. His elongated face was off-center, like a hand-carved piece of art. A nose like a wooden sausage sat in the middle, and he had short tree-branch arms. Sterling would have had to stoop slightly to touch the uppermost leaves on the top of his bushy head. Like most meutes, he could always be found in the company of a wizard.

*He's so little—the size of a piece of luggage but he walks by himself. I know it's wrong to think this, but I want one. Why couldn't I have a meute?*

The potion wizard ignored his grumpy companion just as he had been ignoring Sterling. Instead, he hollowed out a night beetle's innards with the tip of his wand and flicked the gummy blob into the blackened cauldron. Next, his spindly fingers whizzed through the air, directing even more ingredients to float above the brew. Red goo, then glossy black spheres sprinkled into the mix. The magic concoction bubbled over the cauldron's curved edges and gurgled (as did Sterling's stomach).

Sterling watched the flare and fizz in front of him, unsure what to do or say. Then, the potion wizard cupped his hands and wafted the smell of the brew to the tip of his nose.

*Ugh, that smells so horrible and I'm not even standing near it.*

"You're a good cauldron—my loyal friend. I thank the high wizards who brought you from the lava islands all those centuries ago. Ah, the potions we've made together. I do believe the lava spirits are with us today." He grew serious. "I know just what this needs, a dusting of forest moss and a hint—just a drop—of toad's oil."

The thought of toad's oil was terrible enough, but then the musky odor plunged into the air, choking Sterling with oily fumes.

*So gross! I can taste it. Salty grime. Hack!*

Barath pinched his tree-sausage nose with one of

his branches. "This is your most foul-smelling yet! The stench of spoiled mushrooms and toad urine is seeping into my bark. It'll stick for at least a week." He groaned and shook his limbs. "And to think we were lost for days in the forest, all to find the 'perfect' tree root with the 'right' shade of green gunk. I still don't know why all this is so important..."

"Excuse me, sir—" Sterling blurted out, half talking, half coughing.

"In a moment, hunter boy—this is the best part!" the wizard said, without taking his eyes off his cauldron.

Sterling wiped smudges of powder off his face and crossed his arms. He felt out of sorts but tried to look calm and confident. He was getting tired of everyone calling him "boy."

The magic mixture swirled faster at the potion wizard's command. He chanted in another language, one like Elvish but much harsher. His wand scraped against the cauldron, and his chanting boomed. Sterling felt like he would pass out—his senses were perked up and absorbing too much sound and smell.

Sizzling sparks and purple flames leaped from the cauldron; a billow of smoke filled the cave. Barath made gagging noises and spat out splintered bark. Sterling coughed uncontrollably and crouched in hopes of dodging the thickest smoke. Electric fuzz snapped and popped in midair like a display of fresh fireworks until, finally, the sparks dropped to the cave floor in flashes and fizzled out.

*I hate caves for so many reasons—no fresh air, harsh echoes clanging against the stone walls. And I'm less than lukewarm on wizards now too.*

The smell of burnt chemicals was nearly unbearable, and Sterling's vision went black. He craved a fresh breeze and sunshine, tempted to crawl out of the cave if he had to. He thought of the village of Bren.

Back home, Uncle Roag was recovering from dark magic wounds—he suffered a permanent limp and persistent tiredness. Sterling didn't want to be gone for too long. His uncle was the only family he had left, and he was responsible for checking on him. He closed his eyes and wished he were sitting in his uncle's messy food-filled kitchen, a place adorned with odd creatures (he was a talented keeper of rare animals) and his famous hand-drawn maps. Why had the Alin sent him here anyway?

Then, something unexpected happened.

# CHAPTER FIVE

## THE GLASS STONE

The smoke cleared enough to reveal a glowing shape dancing in the potion wizard's half-moon glasses, shining brightly through the haze.

"Isn't she a beauty?!" The potion wizard's smile lifted his beard, making even it look happy. "I'd say we've done it! Don't you agree, boy? A perfect Forest Stone. See here?" Inches from Sterling's face, the potion wizard held a palm-sized translucent stone with a glossy emerald coating.

"It's, um, like magical glass. It's marvelous, sir," Sterling sputtered. He drew himself up, trying to look less like a boy.

The stone gleamed brighter as if it enjoyed the compliment.

Barath waddled over and swatted Sterling's leg just as the young hunter was about to take a step. He fell on his bottom with a thud. He blinked, then decided the grouchy tree had knocked him over by accident.

Barath peered at the glassy stone and arched his wooden eyebrows. "I've seen stones like this before. All they do is bring about all sorts of trouble. Mischief and thievery, I say." He crossed his branches in disapproval before stamping to an oval-shaped nook in the wall. "And I don't expect you, hunter boy, to encourage this nonsense!"

Sterling fidgeted with his cape where the threads were unraveling, unsure how to respond to a talking tree. He didn't want to offend the meute or his master, so he went with a silent nod.

*He knocked me over on purpose. Sneaky little branches!*

"Don't mind him, hunter boy. Barath has never seen a stone like this. He may have lived a thousand years, but his memory and disposition are like a toddler. Tiny meute, not so tiny temper," the potion wizard joked. With a swish of his finger, a spiral of sparkling magic bounced across the cave and tapped the grouchy meute across his top branches.

Barath thrashed his leaves and crossed his trunk. "I will remind you how tall I can grow—we'd see who's tiny! It'd be a rotten day for you if I decided to use my grow magic here in this dingy little cave. I-I'd crack these walls and send the sky shining down. Every other wizard would see what you're up to. Jeanno the Twisted would be mighty curious." Barath stewed. He nestled into the wall's egg-shaped nook until his facial features faded into rigid bark and he appeared like any other tree except quite small.

"He never did have a sense of humor. The old grouch. He hides in his bark without letting me get another word in. Ah, he'll come around, though. He must—"

"I'm sorry, sir, but who is Jeanno the Twisted?" Sterling interrupted. The name sounded like trouble and made the pit of his stomach harden with worry.

The potion wizard wiped his brow with a cloth woven out of pearl thread. Then, for the first time, he looked at Sterling head on. His bright silver, bushy tangled eyebrows were so long they touched the brim of his cap, and his eyes glowed a pale gray around purple pupils.

"A hunter's intuition for detecting danger. I see yours is quite adept. He's a dark wizard. This stone is one of seven that will change the fate of many creatures—and lift Jeanno's curse on them."

Sterling tried not to stare at the wizard's wiry eyebrows when they shifted the wizard's cap for him.

"Yes, sir. Um, I suppose you're right. I'm Sterling Fierce, by the way. My Alin sent me..."

"Ah, yes, the young witch hunter. Your Alin's messenger birds arrived last full moon—what a rowdy flock! They took to arguing with the island blackbirds—caused quite a stir. We're not used to visitors here. I was curious when you'd turn up. Of course, the creatures told me you'd arrived on the island hours ago—they're a chatty bunch, you see."

The potion wizard waved his hands gently in a crisscross, then flicked his wand in a series of up-down motions.

"My condolences for the loss of your father. He was a renowned hunter in his time, but that duty has fallen to you now," the potion wizard said in a heart-felt tone.

"Thank you, sir," Sterling replied.

Calmly, the magical kitchen began to clean up at his command. Cupboards straightened, and a dusty broom hopped along, sweeping mounds of colorful powder into a floating dustpan. There was a hiss as the witch eye was swept to a back corner out of the way.

Sterling plucked an empty glass tube from the floor and rolled it back and forth in his palm. Bits of sparkles glittered inside like an enchanted snow globe.

*Something like this would make a good gift for Uncle Roag.*

"Now, don't touch anything, boy—potion tubes, bottles, mixing spoons are all coated with bits of spells and leftover potions. Strictly speaking, anything lying around here wouldn't hesitate to turn you into a goat or make your hair turn to flaming jelly," he said with a gleeful expression.

Sterling gulped as he set the glass tube of sparkles back onto a shelf. He watched silently as the mixing tools washed themselves with soapy water until the wizard motioned for them to stop. The stone was placed inside a protective box adorned with crystals. Soon, the cave went silent. The potion wizard sat across from his newborn treasure, his eyes fixed on the precious gem.

Sterling sat on a dusty storage chest next to the potion wizard. He wafted smoke remnants away from his face and wished for a glass of clean water.

"I'm sorry. I don't understand what all this means," Sterling admitted. His throat felt drier with every word.

The potion wizard thumped his chest and clutched the stone with ten spindly fingers. He cleared his throat as if he'd been asked to give a speech. "It's mesmerizing to behold—no others like it in this century. Long ago, sure, but those stones were all destroyed. No other wizard could've brought them back. They've tried. Barath is right about one thing. The stones are dangerous in the wrong hands. This must be kept a secret at all costs."

Sterling wished he had something useful to say. Instead, "Mm-hmm" was the best he could offer.

*I don't know why I've been sent here. What am I meant to do?*

Suddenly, a light flashed within the stone's center, and women's voices, speaking in unison, filled the cave: "You have created one of the seven sacred stones, the Forest Stone. The seven sisters of Elm hear your call, Potion Wizard, but six more stones must be forged before our strength returns. The witch hunter will prove useful on your quest—

take him with you and hurry before time escapes us."

*The witch hunter.* Sterling's heart pounded. *How did they know I was here?*

The potion wizard straightened his wizard's cap, extra pointy and tall. Then, he adjusted his glasses in perfect alignment with his pale gray eyes so they didn't slope down his nose anymore.

"Seven Sisters, it would be my great honor to create the seven stones. Together, we must save the dragons and restore balance to the magic realm," the potion wizard said with a bow.

Sterling scanned the cave, but nobody else had come. "Where did those voices come from?"

"I'm afraid I haven't time to explain, hunter boy. We'll need to journey a good distance to collect the ingredients for the second stone. They certainly can't be found around here!" The potion wizard began packing a satchel, stuffing in a map of a mountain range.

"Did the lady—that voice—say...dragons?" Sterling's stomach rumbled with a mix of nerves and hunger. The dryness in his throat still begged for a sip of water.

"Yes, of course, she said dragons! Someone must save them, after all. Jeanno the Twisted—he cursed them into nothingness because he's a dangerous old coward. We must pack light and leave here this instant. Besides, nothing cures a thirst like freshly fallen snow." The potion wizard winked.

"We?" Sterling repeated.

"You heard the sisters, witch hunter. Yes, we go together...oh, and we mustn't forget the grouch!" The potion wizard hoisted a faceless sleeping tree under his arm.

*I suppose 'witch hunter' is an improvement from 'boy,' but I can't go anywhere with him and that devious walking tree trunk! This is crazy. He's crazy—are all wizards this sporadic?*

A corner of the wizard's cape was suddenly draped across Sterling's shoulders, and he was in midflight before he could ask what was happening or make a fuss. In one giant, wobbly wizard's leap over mounds of damp boulders, they flew out of the nameless cave. They skimmed a good number of treetops before dropping into a grassy clearing. Sterling landed on Banefield's back with a gentle thud. Banefield's enchanted horseshoes instantly glowed a fizzy gold and lifted them both off the ground.

"Hey, buddy. I promise this wasn't my idea," Sterling whispered to Banefield, giving the horse his best *I'm sorry, but this wizard is crazy* look.

"And so we begin our quest to undo what Jeanno the Twisted has done," the potion wizard boomed. "Hang on tight, my hunter companion! We aim to be in a hurry!"

Wherever they were going, Sterling knew two things—he wouldn't be going home anytime soon, and he was about to learn about the worst sort of wizard magic.

# CHAPTER SIX
# A DRAGON CALLED GREEN

Snuggled inside a much-too-big dragon's nest slept a creature—an unusual creature. He was an Air Dragon child with gleaming emerald scales from head to tail and a round and very green belly. Snores roared from his bedroom, but the rest of the house was as silent as the forest in the deep of night. Dragon snorts bounced off stone walls and slipped through the ceiling window to be heard for miles by the hunting owls and other nocturnal scavengers.

Like most Air Dragon homes, this one had a magical sloped roof made of one giant piece of carved glass that swooped outward smoothly and glistened in the moonlight. These enchanted roofs, or "sky windows," allowed the sky- and wind-loving dragons to enjoy views of the heavens as often as possible.

The little dragon's room was filled with a construct of branches and vines lined with bird fluff and soft hay to create a nest. When he breathed in, feathers were sucked into his dark, cave-like nostrils before darting back out with each exhale. Drenched in dragon snot and too heavy to float, a few stray feathers plummeted down to the dragon's green belly, sticking like gooey snowflakes onto a grassy hill.

"Three prickly plum pies, please. Um—and one super-big tangerine meat shake with an extra scoop of salt cream." The dragon child licked his lips, and his pointy white teeth slipped out. In his sleep, he gnawed on nest twigs hanging too close to his scaly nose and mouth. The worn sticks were riddled with old bite marks and slobber stains.

As the sun crested the horizon, light flooded the bedroom, spilling in from the sky window. One dragon eye sprang open, then snapped shut.

"Too bright," he groaned.

A blur of emerald scales flashed as he rolled over, and blue cotton-candy-like hair plunged into the middle of the nest. A cyclone of nest feathers whirled into a spinning cloud. Some floated downward, scattering across the bare floor and nestling into the soft dirt without making a sound. Soon, bird chatter was too loud to ignore, and the dragon child stirred. A deep yawn shook the nest, and triangular tail scales flexed and scratched his head.

A toothy grin flashed across his face. "Don't forget behind the horns."

His tail nodded in agreement and did as he said.

"That's the spot!" He sighed with relief, then

stretched his wings. "When did I eat a whole bird?" he wondered aloud, giving a knowing glance at his tail.

"You know what to do."

His plump tail swung toward his face. It stopped inches from giving his snout a good bashing. Instead, it flossed strands of feather fluff from between his teeth using the thinnest tail scale.

Besides his grand size and mouthful of sharp teeth, the dragon child had a friendly appearance. His name was Green, as he was the only green-scaled dragon; the name was a natural fit. He was also the only dragon that walked to school each day, watching the others soar over him in the sky.

As a very young dragon, Green would complain to his parents, "All the dragons at school can fly—even the littlest dragons. And Jerimi Spinetail soars up into the clouds for a long time. He can breathe out storm winds too! I saw him blow three dragons clear across the cafeteria! I can't do anything like that. I can't do any normal dragon things."

The calm words of his mother were always the same: "Green, you are a special dragon. One day, your magic will come." Her honey-brown eyes were always full of love. Green wanted so badly to believe her.

"That's right," his father would echo. "You are just as much a dragon as the rest of your friends—you look like a dragon, eat like a dragon, live like a dragon. That's what matters."

In the still morning light, his home felt too quiet. No breakfast-being-made-for-him noises were coming from the kitchen, no scuffling around from his dad's heavy footsteps or dragon tail thumping along the dirt floor. Even the smell of hot chocolate (a dragon's favorite morning beverage) was missing. Green catapulted himself out of his nest. He stood in front of a mirror bordered with seashells and mud crystals. Sparkling eyes, a mix of amber and emerald-green splashes, stared back at him. He tugged a bark comb through unruly hair puffs. Strands of powder blue bounced right back out of place after each stroke, like misshapen springs too stubborn to straighten.

"It's no use. I'm a silly-looking, green land monster —and now my hair looks sloppy."

His tail tilted its tip to the side and shook from side to side.

Green shuffled down the arched hallway. His tail tapped against the brick walls and left behind light scratch marks. These markings started at the bottom of the bricks from when he was a baby dragon and reached halfway up to the ceiling. But he felt small in this hallway, no matter how much he grew.

The hallway was extra dark this morning. The house mice didn't scamper around for food, and his mom hadn't lit the candles hanging from the sturdy wooden beams above. Instead, spheres made from thin bone, filled with cold hard wax, were nearly swallowed in darkness. A sense of worry washed over him, but he pressed on. His sparkling emerald eyes peeked around the corner, but the kitchen was dreadfully empty.

*We're low on meat pie. Maybe they went out for a last-minute hunt?*

The dome-shaped ceiling was infused with enchantments to function like one-way glass. The dragon family could see out, but nobody could see inside. While something wasn't quite right inside, outside, it looked like a typical day, and the sun's angle meant it was time to leave for school. He slurped down the last of the sheep's milk and gobbled down leftover ham pies and sour cherry tarts. Then, he licked his face clean and slipped on a hand-me-down purple vest that had been his father's. It was stitched all over with a moon and stars pattern. They could glow in darkness, but only when they wanted to.

Green scribbled a note to his parents in his best handwriting to explain that he'd gone to school, the famous WinFire Academy for Dragons, where dragons trained on dragon skills (fire breathing, flying, and magic history lessons). Of course, it wasn't only for dragon students. The occasional witch, wizard, or seemingly ordinary human attended classes, but most didn't stay long.

# CHAPTER SEVEN

# DISAPPEARANCE OF THE DRAGONS

G reen's emergency stash of dracoins jiggled with only two or three pieces, hardly enough to buy lunch. Sometimes the school had leftovers for a bargain. If not, Professor Dwaye, a wizard from the ice lands with a beard full of snow crystals, usually snuck something from the staff kitchen. "I know all about being hungry, my boy. In the iciest season, we'd starve if we didn't help one another. I know you dragons need a lot to fill your bellies. I can't promise that'll happen, but you won't starve on my watch," Professor Dwaye had said once when he'd found Green crying over a stolen lunch.

"Dragons will be dragons," his professor had said. But Green wasn't sure what the professor meant. Certainly, not all dragons had a mean streak. Green had never stolen anyone's lunch or made fun of other dragons when they cast the wrong spell or crash-landed. But then again, he was different from the other dragons.

On the way to the edge of the Spakar Mountains, a breeze cooled his scales, and he stopped worrying about his parents' whereabouts. He told himself they were fine, and he rang the bell for the flajicks to take him across the water to WinFire Academy. The flajicks' long beaks pierced through the layer of fog that hovered over the water. It hadn't dissipated yet, hidden in the mountain's shadow. The flajicks used paddle-like wings to navigate the current as they had for centuries. The giant birds could easily carry an adult dragon between the two of them. Since Green couldn't fly, he was the only dragon that crossed the water this way. They pulled him across toward the school's floating island. A V formation of seabirds whizzed overhead. He heard seabird laughter and wished he could turn invisible.

*Go ahead and keep flying. Laugh at the silly land dragon.*

Soon, the giant waterbirds reached the stone path leading to the academy. Glowing signs in dragon language warned trespassers not to enter.

*Private Dragon School Premises* one sign read. *Windstorm-Breathers Above and Below. Not Responsible for Injuries or Peril* read another.

Green turned back to the graceful birds.

"Thanks for the ride, as always." He tossed bread chunks from his vest pocket and flashed a toothy grin. His eyes twinkled pure emerald.

Sharp beaks detected the food with pinpoint accuracy and swallowed the chunks whole. A hacking sound followed, then a squawk that hopefully meant they were satisfied with their payment. Their feathers ruffled and then settled down smoothly as the birds paddled away.

Green had arrived on time, but no dragons were gathered outside the academy's entrance, and no dragons peered down from the cafe deck. A feeling of dread washed over him as he realized something wasn't right—not at home, and not at school. In fact, there were no other dragons anywhere.

He poked his fluffy-topped head into the kitchens (there were four of them) where no breakfast had been prepared. No fires had been lit, and dusty onions sat in overflowing crates. Potato sacks were secured with packaging twine. Only a few lumpy brown spuds poured onto the floor, waiting to be transformed into a stew or mashed into a thick pie filling. Bundles of raw wheat were untouched. No bread dough baked in the giant clay ovens, and the fire spits were bare.

A coldness tingled in Green's tail.

Meat bones were usually roasting well before the sun rose. Nothing looked right.

Next, he roamed through the library. He'd never seen the reading room empty before, and there was no librarian with smudged glasses and ink-stained claws. The copiers didn't hum and clank like usual. The potion-brewing room was empty too; the fire ring exercise course—desolate. Swim holes and sky loops and the great hunting forest were all dragonless.

Green hurried out of the academy. He fetched a flajick ride north and took the long way around the Evertwine River. There were no dragons to be seen from the riverway to the sea or along any trail he tracked. Next, he checked the caves, treehouses, and nesting homes of every dragon he knew, tapping the doors with his plump tail and hollering out his best dragon calls. But there were only empty homes with the usual things in their familiar places.

It was as if every dragon had disappeared in the middle of the night—every dragon except Green.

He wondered about his parents and if they'd not gone hunting after all. Finally, he walked back toward his village.

"Squeak, squawk, stop!" screamed a tiny raccoon.

Green stumbled backward and landed on his belly. He bounced forward and came face-to-face with eight scruffy raccoons.

"I'm sorry. I-I didn't see you on the path," Green apologized, his eyes changing quickly to a dull shade of amber.

The tallest of the raccoons stood tall and glared down at Green. "We scamper and sneak at everyone's feet, always afraid of being squashed. It's only fair that you dragons pay attention to where you're going—or whom you're stepping on! You have wings—go fly and let us have the land paths, Air Dragon!"

Green frowned with embarrassment and dusted

himself off. He wished more than anything that he could fly.

The raccoons scurried out of sight and off the main path.

"Wait, have you seen any dragons today?" Green called out.

But there was no answer. Green went home to think about what to do, and it wasn't long before his dragon's instinct led him to a full-scale hunt in his living room.

*The answer's here—somewhere in one of these books.*

He scavenged the bookshelves and tossed aside cooking books and carved dragon-tooth knick-knacks. One of the books called to him with a pulsing buzz, but he didn't know which one. Soon, the air was full of dust, and a pile of books stood as high as the ceiling. After scanning a good number of them, Green found one that clicked and chimed as soon as it touched his thick green paws. He turned the book over, inspecting it front to back. Dust trickled from its leather cover like sand in an hourglass. The title appeared in golden letters, *The Potion Wizard's Mixtures of Magic.*

He sniffed its pages. "Syrup and stale ink. Not the worst smell in Everen."

The book told of a powerful potion wizard who helped other creatures, especially in defense against evil magic doers and harmful spells. Green knew that dragons weren't welcome in all parts of Everen—and one group of wizards wished dragons to be gone altogether.

Long ago, the Ottomon Wizards had accused dragons of holding too much power and had used magic to banish them. Green shivered, remembering his mother's stories about the cruelty dragons had suffered at the hands of the Ottomon Wizards. Some of their horns had been removed, tails broken, and worse—anything to try to stop their magical powers. But the famous potion wizard had saved the dragons, fighting against the dark wizards.

"I know what I have to do," he said. His tail nodded in agreement.

Green packed the last meat pies and the wizard book. Their pet caracal, Shadow, grumbled at the commotion. Her pointy black ears stirred from the corner of the room. He'd forgotten she was hidden in the shadows—true to her name. She purred and scrunched her whiskers. Then, she blinked at his leather satchel as if she understood he was leaving. Green laid down a meat pie for her and ran his tail across her furry back.

"I'm off to find the potion wizard. He can help me find Mom and Dad—and all the dragons. I won't let anyone down, Shadow, dragon's promise," he whispered before stepping out, closing the heavy stone door behind him.

## CHAPTER EIGHT

# A SNOWY HIKE AND A
# GRUMPY LITTLE TREE

Patches of dense forest and ocean waves flashed beneath Sterling like vivid green-and-blue quilt pieces haphazardly stitched together. The flight over the Isles of Grunne had been windy, and the winter sea was choppy as usual. Nevertheless, the salty air had been refreshing, and the wind blew in their favor most of the journey.

Once Banefield calmed down and stopped panicking, Sterling found riding a flying horse exhilarating. The potion wizard's flying spell was potent, cast on already-enchanted horseshoes. If not, Banefield would have landed immediately. He didn't take to the skies willingly, but magic has a way of bending even the most stubborn of creatures. Sterling himself didn't mind how the clouds whipped through his hair and flapped fresh air beneath his cape.

He patted the horse's neck and circled his fingertips in his fur. "See, boy? It isn't so bad up here," Sterling said.

Banefield snorted and shook his mane the way he did when he didn't get his favorite honey apples at the market.

"We'll soon reach the Artison Mountain Range. Do you know of them, hunter boy?" the potion wizard hollered in the wind.

Sterling nodded. "Yes. My father—all hunters know them as the White Mountains."

The potion wizard chuckled. "Yes, that they are!"

Before long, the salt left the air, replaced by frigid specks of snow. Clouds swirled like gray soup. The potion wizard led them closer to the Artison Mountains, never consulting a map or slowing for a moment. He seemed focused or worried, Sterling couldn't tell which. Even Barath piped down for the flight. They reached the base of the mountains and found a safe place for Banefield to rest. Then, the potion wizard, Barath, and Sterling traveled by foot, ascending a snow-covered trail that wound up the mountain. It was steep in places and narrow. There would've been no room for a horse, Sterling noted.

It wasn't long before Barath returned to his grumbling. "I don't know why your spell calls for pristine mountain snow. Wouldn't any snow do? It's deathly cold up here. I could lose my leaves, you know." His wooden teeth chattered with a clunking sound before he leaped onto the potion wizard's shoulder, where he perched like a funny-looking tree parrot.

"Now, don't even think about rooting on me. You'd ruin a perfectly good wizard's cape. The enchantments won't be much use if you poke your ol' branches through," the potion wizard warned, tugging at the loose material that drooped around his neck before enchanting a piece of it to swaddle Barath.

"Hmph," the meute replied, which Sterling assumed was restrained gratitude for the wizard using his magic energy to make him more comfortable.

The potion wizard's staff sparked with each strike against the frozen ground, chock-full of magic, Sterling guessed. He kept pace with the wizard's impressive stride but not without slipping on concealed ice patches occasionally.

"Ow!" Sterling dodged a pine branch but couldn't escape its sharp pine needles.

"Mind the trees. They have feelings too," Barath scolded.

"I didn't mean to—besides, I'm the one that got hurt," Sterling said, finally standing his ground with the meute.

"Tree was there first, hunter boy!" the meute retorted, sticking out his tongue, which looked more like a crumpled piece of brown butcher paper.

Sterling wanted to spout off an insult or two, but he remembered the wizard's mention about meutes acting like toddlers.

*I'm not going to argue with a tree, even a mean little tree.*

Before long, they'd climbed halfway up the mountain. Under the pale clouds, shades of white blanketed every inch of the place, making it hard to tell the land from the sky.

"There's more snow here than anywhere I've ever seen. It's...beautiful," Sterling whispered.

Even the potion wizard slowed long enough to take in the arctic scenery. "I've found, in my long life, that such beauty does not exist without a measure of danger. These mountains would be fatal for most creatures. But, ah—what a sight!"

The mountain rock, streaked with hues of purple and brown, peeked from beneath the snow. Puffy-tailed squirrels darted from limb to limb searching for food, and albino hares with pure white lashes blinked at the passersby.

"It's worth the hike, sir," Sterling said in a voice that sounded like his father's, commanding but kind.

"Oh? I'd prefer the quiet woods..." Barath put in, "or the beach—somewhere with plenty of sunshine. Anywhere but here, but what does my opinion count for? Hmph." Barath spoke without moving his mouth. His bark stiffened from the dropping temperature, making him sound grumpier, if that was possible.

"The white-tipped range is famous for its year-long snow. Its peaks are visible for many miles and home to rare and beautiful creatures," the potion wizard said, ignoring the grouchy meute on his shoulder.

The higher they climbed, the more Sterling understood why Barath opposed the mountains so much. His clothing was useless against the mountain wind. It blew down on them and from the sides like an invisible metal zipper whipping against his body. His cape was woven from thick cloth and bear hide, but now it was coated with pure, white snow—inches of it. At least whenever he was thirsty, snowflakes landed happily in his mouth. They tasted sweet, like the freshest river water imaginable but melted with haste.

*Banefield would've liked to munch on this snow. I hope he's okay down there.*

Sterling missed his loyal travel companion, but he was thankful the potion wizard had insisted that Banefield stay at the mountain's base. After all, the steep incline, frigid gusts, and loose rock weren't fit for a horse, even one as grand as Banefield. Besides, he'd have been annoyed with Barath and his bickering with the wizard. Banefield had tolerated a plendi on their first quest. She was a half fairy, half plant full of magic sparkles and bossiness. But the horse hadn't taken a liking to these new magic beings, not even a little. He'd been enchanted into flying over Everen without warning, and Barath seemed to him little more than a talking tree with leaves off-limits for grazing; how disappointing for a horse.

## CHAPTER NINE
# THE SEARCH FOR GLOWING SNOW

As they continued up the mountain, the wind grew colder and colder. The potion wizard had asked the meute to walk for a bit when he got too heavy, but as they continued, Barath took to moaning pitiably.

"Oh, grumpus," the potion wizard chided. "Look around—the other trees thrive in the cold! Besides, this view is most spectacular! It's worth the bout of frosty weather, I say." He pressed on. He didn't seem to notice the snow pelting his pointed cap or the icicles clinking together in his long silver beard.

Sterling's eyes widened as he watched strands of the wizard's hair shuffle into thin sections and braid themselves.

*Even his hair is enchanted.*

Then, the wizard's robe, cap, and body turned translucent, blending in with the wintery scenery like snow snuggling into mountain nooks as if it had always been there.

Sterling knew that wizards were bonded with the forces of nature, but he'd never seen wizard magic in person. It was a sight to behold, even for the young witch hunter.

The northern wind blew stronger as they climbed the mountain. A whistling cried out from high up the mountaintop.

"Nobody should be this close to the howling peaks," Barath muttered. "I don't have a good feeling about this. No, not at all." His leaves had changed from bright green to pumpkin orange midway up the mountain. Now, they were splashed with a burnt crimson hue. Some had crumpled into brown, shrunken bits. "The arctic wind is too much, oh-all-knowing one. I'm going to lose all my leaves!" He hugged his trunk with his nearly bare branches and whimpered.

The potion wizard sighed without glancing at his talking tree companion. "A bit of fresh air and mountain snow is healthy for you. Yes, those leaves may go. You'll sprout nicer ones, or perhaps lovely, scented flowers will bloom in their place. Wouldn't that be a welcome change, Barath?"

"Flowers? Humph. Not in a thousand years have I sprouted flowers. If these escapades chasing down these silly stones somehow turn me into a bouquet, I'll turn you into a meute," Barath threatened. "Then you'd know how losing leaves feels. It's a shameful business."

"All bark and no bite, my old friend," the wizard retorted with a chuckle.

Sterling mustered a half smile and wrapped the fold of the wizard's cape around Barath, whose wooden teeth chattered relentlessly. He didn't feel friendly toward Barath, especially after his tantrums and rude remarks, but he didn't want him to be in pain either.

Suddenly, the potion wizard stopped walking. He propped himself upright, tall and straight with his staff. Sterling hadn't noticed its details before, but the wooden staff was on display now that the wizard was nearly invisible.

"Wow, sir—are those...troll teeth?" Sterling gasped.

"Why yes, boy. There aren't many who live to tell of a troll encounter, let alone identify troll teeth, I'm afraid. Trolls are a nasty bunch," the potion wizard said, rotating his staff toward Sterling.

"Have you?" The wizard asked as he eyed Sterling. "Encountered a troll before?"

Sterling snorted as he laughed. "Oh, no, sir. Just in books—my father kept a lot of books, and I sort of— have a memory for things that are deadly," he explained.

"Ah yes, inborn hunter instincts—to perceive threats and know your enemies. It's a cumbersome responsibility to see the world that way, but that's what makes hunters different. Go ahead, have a look," the wizard nodded.

"Thank you—it's unusual—nice, I mean," Sterling said, running his gloved hand over the enchanted jungle wood. It bent in a crooked twist of dark purple and black strands, glittering in places where tiny gold stars were sprinkled into the wood. At its base were jagged yellow troll teeth, only smooth on the bottom where they'd pounded against the ground for hundreds of years. He recognized the troll teeth from storybook pictures—except they were surprisingly massive, making him aware of how tiny he was compared to such beasts.

"A full-grown troll must be monstrous in person," Sterling said.

"Yes, they are. And troll teeth are stronger than rock—trolls eat boulders and chew up rocks when they're out of meat, so they've evolved to have the strongest teeth of any creature. A family of trolls will devour a herd of sheep or horses if they catch them. But, for the sake of the livestock, trolls are slow as molasses and dim-witted—vicious even to each other."

"I never thought I'd feel sorry for a bunch of rocks, but I sort of do after seeing the size of those chompers. I hope I never meet a troll—not up close, anyway," Sterling said. As the words dropped out of his mouth, he realized that the potion wizard knew too much about trolls never to have met one.

"No, I hope not for your sake either. Rock eaters

do not belong among decent creatures. Would you like to hear the secret to defeating a troll?" the wizard asked, piquing Sterling's interest.

Sterling's eyes widened. "I would," he admitted.

"Run fast and don't look in their eyes. They have a hypnotic gaze that can turn you to stone, temporarily," the wizard said in a hushed voice as he struck the staff against the mountain rock and continued upward.

Sterling wondered what other creatures the wizard had seen in his long life—probably more than Sterling had time to hear about. Despite Sterling's instinct not to trust magical creatures right away, he was impressed when the potion wizard freely shared his knowledge. And the wizard had used his magic energy purely to comfort Barath. Wizards could only use limited amounts of magical energy before they needed to recharge. The older the wizard, the more energy he could hold. This was lucky—or unlucky, depending on the wizard's intentions. But for now, Sterling decided that the potion wizard meant well.

"There it is! The glowing snow of the White Mountains! It's magnificent! I've never seen anything like it in all my time." The potion wizard beamed as he peered through an extended sightseer device. Its goldish metal tube widened at the end, where a bit of glass bubbled out. "It'll be a tricky climb. I'll return when I can—take shelter until then." He turned to go but whirled back.

"Oh yes—I'd nearly forgotten!" The wizard heaved

something toward Sterling. It tumbled through the air and nearly soared over his head, but Sterling jumped reflexively and snatched it out of the air before it could disappear into the snow. It was Barath.

*Whew! Good catch, Fierce.*

"Keep an eye on mister grouchy limbs, if you would be so kind, hunter boy," the wizard's voice trailed off.

"Wait!" Sterling begged. But it was no use. The potion wizard's footprints sank into the mountain snow higher and farther away until they were out of sight.

It was then that whatever thread of luck he had unraveled. The wind howled, and a sky full of snow blew in faster than any rain back home. A storm of white swirled around him in seconds, and there was no stopping it.

# CHAPTER TEN
## A WIZARD'S WAVE

"It's a blizzard—get movin' or we'll be buried in it!" a familiar voice nagged.

Sterling looked down at the object cradled in his arms and was met with a human-like stare beneath wooden eyelids. The young witch hunter took a deep breath and scanned the mountainside, activating his heat-seeking sight. Unlike the wizard's magic energy, Sterling's hunter abilities only surfaced when he needed them, so he could only learn to use them when he was already in danger.

*Focus, Fierce. Really focus. Which way do we go?*

A grove of trees glowed red, which meant that spot was either warm or dry—either option was better than being out in the open where blasts of snow were already pummeling him. He carried the misshapen trunk on his shoulders like a sack of pecans, then like a babe. Branches poked him no matter what position he tried.

*How does the wizard carry this heavy little guy? Probably uses magic from his cape—wizards have all the fancy stuff.*

Just then, an arctic explosion thundered behind him. An avalanche hurled enormous ship-sized heaps of snow down the mountain. White, powdery waves crashed and demolished the trail he'd stood on moments earlier. He trudged through the waist-deep drifts toward the grove of trees as fast as his cold, numb legs could carry him. Every time he thought he was closer, another burst of white blinded him.

"C'mon, hunter's sight. Show me the trees one more time!" Sterling begged.

Thankfully, a red light flickered from nearby. It took most of Sterling's strength, but he reached the grove. It was smaller than he'd hoped, but it would have to do. Using a hunter's shelter-building technique, he constructed an arched space from tree limbs and stones, then "glued" them together by thawing snow in his hands, then smashing it onto the joints, where it froze almost instantly. He cleared the snow away from a tree stump, but the soil was frozen and nearly as cold and hard as a rock, so he pulled a few pine branches into the shelter to sit on and lugged Barath to it.

"This should shield us from the brunt of the storm, but it blew away the wizard's cape he made for you," Sterling explained.

He braced for an insult. But instead, wooden teeth chattered, then went silent.

It didn't matter that his fingers and toes were numb—he started to worry more about Barath. The tiny tree could no longer walk or move at all. His limbs had frozen stiff, and his wooden face drooped with the weight of icicles. When his eyes drifted to meet Sterling's, a deepness stared back. It was a deepness that only resided in creatures who'd experienced many lifetimes. It reminded Sterling of the golden-orange eyes of the great protector of Everen, the Red Wolf—and even the witches he'd encountered. Witches, as evil as they were, lived for centuries and longer. They, too, bore the telltale deepness that long life brought.

"Wizards. Why do I befriend wizards?" Barath finally whimpered. His wooden teeth made a faint *clunk-clunk-clunk* sound. Sterling frowned. It seemed odd that the wizard would leave without Barath. He'd thought meutes only left their wizards in dire emergencies.

"Will you be okay—I mean, if you lose all of your leaves?" Sterling asked, unsure what this meant for the tiny tree being. He unlatched his own cap and wrapped it snuggly around Barath, mimicking how he'd seen mothers comfort their children.

"Oh, that's not up to me, boy..." Barath's voice trailed off. "Destiny and nature...my part is done when they say it is. But you can choose a different path."

Sterling's stone-gray eyes swirled like a brewing storm.

"What can I do? Barath! Tell me how to help!"

In seconds, Barath's tiny face faded into ordinary-looking bark. His leaves shriveled and loosened one by one, blowing away in the snowstorm.

Sterling cradled the ice-cold tree and waited for the potion wizard. He had to return soon—unless he was caught out in the storm or worse.

Blizzard winds blew snow in every direction, angrier than before. The howling peaks were true to their name. At first, there were low howls, but they grew louder, more piercing.

*The snow leopard.*

He recalled stories his father had told on winter nights—stories of the arctic beast that protected the snow lands. Her howls were legendary. But they were just stories, weren't they?

Suddenly, a shouting disturbed the silence.

"Don't just sit there! We must move down the mountain—now! This hut won't hold—not against what's coming!" The potion wizard hurtled toward them, huffing, and crashing into the makeshift shelter. He shoved Barath into his wizard's cap and nodded.

"Join me, boy," he gestured with an outreached hand. "A wizard's wave is tumultuous, but it'll get us down!"

Sterling hesitated—this wasn't the time to insist on a more dignified title than boy—then gripped the potion wizard's hand. Surprisingly, it wasn't frozen or even wet from the snow. The wizard's grip seemed to pull the frozen particles from Sterling's clothes and hair. Ice droplets rose all around them and zipped in circles, then snapped together in swirling lumps. Tiny blue sparks formed a giant wave of glowing snow, and a blanket of wiggly air currents swept beneath their feet.

*Wow, he can manipulate the elements*, he thought with excitement as a boyish grin crossed his face.

Next, a flurry of snowflakes forged a sphere around them as the booming sounds of the avalanche grew louder.

"Downward to the mountain's low! Wizard's wave, we go!" he cried out. His words echoed off the mountain peaks like they had in the nameless cave.

Then, the magical wave began to crash down the mountain, carrying them with it. It jolted and pulled faster than any horse ride. In their wake, they left dented bushes, snapped branches, and a strange, curved impression in the snow.

Even after his lips went numb from the cold, Sterling mustered a stiff smile as they sped down the decline.

*A snow wave! And I'm riding it!*

# CHAPTER ELEVEN
# HOWLING PEAKS

"Hang on, boy! Best prepare for a bumpy landing!" the potion wizard exclaimed.

Sterling winced as he looked around. They'd only made it halfway down the mountain. He made up his mind to address the topic of the wizard calling him "boy" after they'd landed—if that was indeed what they were trying to do. Thrashing about and nearly losing their balance, they slammed to a stop. A splash of ice glittered in the air, then the wizard's wave disappeared.

"This is as far as I can take us for now," the potion wizard huffed. "Can you hike down the rest of the way? We have little time before the blizzard catches up."

"Um, yeah," Sterling sputtered. He spun, trying to make eye contact with the wizard, but snow flurries stuck to his lashes like icy glue.

The wizard sighed. "You need rest—I could use

some too." He poked piles of snow with his staff. "I always lose my glasses on those waves..." With a flick of his wand, spectacles sprung from the snow. The smudged half-moon lenses floated up to rest on his oversized nose.

"Ah yes, there," he pointed toward a small opening in the mountain a few steps away. "It's a tiny cave, but it's good enough until the blizzard passes," the potion wizard said. "Now, let's go settle in."

"A wolf's den? Are you mad?" exclaimed Barath, peering out from under the wizard's cap.

Sterling grinned, thankful that Barath was okay—he didn't mind that the little tree was back to his feisty self.

"There is no other choice. I'm afraid the blizzard is a beastly one, and I've run short of magic energy. Our young hunter is not made of bark—we will rest in the warm, dry cave." The potion wizard lowered the little tree to the ground. "You're welcome to root out here in the cold, but I warn you, there are worse creatures than wolves in these parts," he remarked, before ducking inside.

Sterling followed without hesitation. Every inch of his clothing was drenched. Ice prickles formed on his cape and stung his back. He couldn't feel his legs, much less the insides of his boots—he'd forgotten he even had toes. His body ached, and his mind was fuzzy. It was a miracle his legs still moved.

With a flick of the wizard's wand, a soft green flame lit up the inside of the cave. There were no wolves in sight, thankfully. The cave was small, and patches of straw and leaves showed signs of makeshift bedding.

"Potion Wizard, sir, there are beds for a pack of animals here, and some there too," Sterling whispered. He hoped he wouldn't have to explain further. He was fatigued and losing more energy with every word.

Instead of quizzing him, the potion wizard poked and prodded the cave floor with his staff.

*Clack-clack-clack.*

More tiny green flames snapped on, lighting the darkness the way glow flies did in the thick of the swamplands.

Spying from behind a boulder at the cave's entrance, Barath called inside.

"Oh, c'mon. I can smell wet fur from here. They'll be back, you know. Our best hope is that they're stranded in this snow spectacle. If we're lucky, we stay in a flea-infested hole. If we're unlucky, I'm as good as a slobbery fetching stick for a pack of dim-witted wolf cubs by morning," Barath said in his grouchiest tone yet. Still, he wobbled inside.

The potion wizard cast a knowing grin.

"Wolves are wiser than they let on. It is foolish to underestimate any creature, Barath. The hunter boy knows." The potion wizard's wand pointed at hay bedding. "What do you think, hunter?"

"Yes, sir. They live in a pack. Together, they have

the strength—knowledge—to survive even in the cold," Sterling said through chattering teeth.

"It takes intelligence to work as a pack and more thinking and brainpower than you'd imagine, you ol' grouch," the potion wizard said. His wand danced a few beats and sorted hay into piles.

Sterling shoved clumps of dried leaves into a makeshift pillow and curled into a ball the way he had as a young child. He was too cold, too tired to do anything else. His eyes closed.

When he woke hours later, it was to the most comforting sound—the cracking of a cooking fire. Thanks to some wizardry, a bit of rabbit stew and an acorn medley had been conjured up for dinner.

Barath snuggled into the hay and warmed his roots by the fire with a yawn. "I suppose I've had worse accommodations alongside the great potion wizard." He half smiled.

"Well, old boy, it pleases me that something is to your liking. I was beginning to think you'd had enough of my adventure chasing. I worry a day will come when you no longer wish to journey with me. I'd be a grumpy old goat out here on my own," he chuckled.

Despite their bickering, Sterling sensed how much the meute and the potion wizard meant to each other. And he realized how much he enjoyed their company. It was an unexpected family feeling, but it was comforting, especially far from home.

"How long have you two been adventuring?" Sterling asked with a yawn.

"More centuries than he'd like," the potion wizard admitted. "But there are many mysteries and magics in Everen still waiting to be discovered."

A blood-curdling howl rang from the mountaintops and reverberated inside the small cave.

"The snow leopard!" Sterling blurted out instinctively. A tingle ran down his spine as his hand grasped his dagger.

"No, no," the potion wizard said with certainty.

"Not the howling—that's a wolf's howl. The snow leopard is hunting them," Sterling whispered with a detectable sadness.

"She must've found the wolves from this cave when they ventured out for food and were stranded in the blizzard. Her hunger grows strongest in the colder season. It's dangerous to be out when she's hunting—even for a pack of wolves," the potion wizard said with a mixture of sorrow and relief.

Sterling thought of the legendary Red Wolf, Everen's great protector. Wolves were dangerous when provoked, but they were also noble and loyal creatures worthy of deep respect.

"We should help them," Sterling said.

"Now, this is the snow leopard's home, and she must protect it. The wolves play their part in the wilds of nature. We're fortunate she allowed us to pass through unharmed and uneaten. She is mighty and ancient."

"Like you?" Sterling probed.

The potion wizard smiled and then puffed on a long, wooden pipe. Lavender-scented smoke seeped out and swirled delicately in the air.

"Yes, hunter boy. In a way."

If the snow leopard was like the potion wizard, what did that make the wolves?

"Potion Wizard, sir," Sterling began, "why am I here? I'm sorry, but I don't understand why—"

"You are here because you are meant to be. What is your purpose? You have the gift of blood magic, do you not?"

"I do have the gift. I mean, I thought I was a normal hunter until my blood started shooting arrows and things. My father hid me in Bren, far from most magic doers of any kind, and he kept my iden-tity secret—even from me. He was killed before he had a chance to teach me," Sterling said. Even after all this time, his voice still caught and his eyes welled when he spoke about his father aloud.

"Yes, I'm awfully sorry for your circumstances. Sadly, mortal lives are often unfinished. But tell me, what is the purpose of witch hunters?"

"We fight witches that go dark—take too much power and harm others," Sterling said.

"And your blood magic—these powers can destroy witches. What do you think the witches will do if the wizards successfully destroy their powerful foes, the dragons? They will follow—band together with the dark wizards."

"Can't we just talk to these wizards and come to some kind of agreement? What do these stones even do?" Sterling peered at the potion wizard, suddenly mistrustful again. "I'm sure if we just talked, we could come up with some sort of compromise," he suggested.

The wizard gasped as if Sterling's words profoundly offended him.

"You do not know powerful magic and what it does to those that hold it. Power always seeks more power. The dark wizards and witches will spark a war that will tear Everen apart. Magic doers against those who threaten them! Can't you understand, boy?"

Sterling glanced at the dagger tucked neatly into his leather belt. The potion wizard had been around for a long time, but surely he didn't mean to harm the dark wizards. But you never knew with the magic ones.

"I'm sorry, I just hoped—" he started.

"There is no hope for what and who we are dealing with. An attack on magical creatures is an attack on those who stand for balance. It is an attack on all of us—on me, and on you, Sterling Fierce."

The potion wizard stayed awake late into the night, examining the White Mountain snow he'd collected. Sterling stared at the magical substance for so long that he saw it when he closed his eyes. It was preserved within a thin, translucent bubble that flashed rainbow hues and spun slowly. White light danced across its surface as if somehow it were alive.

Barath snored from the corner of the wolf's den. Sap dripped from his wooden mouth, and he looked irritated even as he slept. Emerald-hued flames flickered in the fire ring, revealing tiny scars on limbs where leaves had sprouted.

The potion wizard glanced over and cleared his throat. "Some battles are worth the agony of nature's fury and a bit of frost," he whispered in a fatherly tone toward Barath, before tilting his head toward Sterling. "Especially this battle. You'll see soon enough, young hunter. Trust me."

A ball of worry and excitement rolled around in Sterling's stomach. Something important was coming —something big. But could he really trust the potion wizard?

# CHAPTER TWELVE
# THE MOUNTAIN STONE

During the return flight over the Sea of Grunne, Sterling's face and fingers (and toes) finally thawed. After spending the night in a wolf's den, he didn't mind the wizard's cave as much. Even the smell of frog oil and burnt feathers offended his senses less. It was certainly warmer than the White Mountains, and they were as good as a million miles away from the blizzard—and the snow leopard. Although, her howls still echoed in the back of his skull. He had a strange feeling he'd see her one day—the notion was terrifying and alluring all at once.

Ingredients floated through the air and poured into the potion wizard's bubbling brew. A particularly loud pop startled Sterling. He placed his hand on his sheathed dagger out of habit.

"A splash of blizzard's fury and one troll's spoonful of cold mountain stone—depending on the size of the troll," the potion wizard said. He danced around his mixing station, an ordinary wooden spoon in one hand and his wand in the other.

*This is where he's truly happy*, Sterling thought. He was somewhat envious that the wizard found happiness in potion-making—the thing he was destined to do. Sterling had slain witches on his quests, the thing he was meant for, but it hadn't made him happy.

"My brew is almost complete! Two stones will be ready. Five more to go. I miss the dragons dearly, even if some are troublesome or downright deadly. Alas, it'd be boring without dragons. Everen wouldn't be the same." The potion wizard's voice trailed off as though his mind were slipping into memories of dragons.

Since returning to the cave without a name, Barath had not left his oval-shaped nook in the wall, avoiding the brewing potion. Instead, he sipped warm sap from a mug and sporadically jolted his limbs, popping blue-and-white flashes on and off. The light was painfully bright to Sterling, but the potion wizard called these "tree shivers" and said to pay no attention to them.

"My bark is frozen from the inside out. Even the boy has a fur hide and cape to protect him, and he's been a wizard's companion for a few days. I follow you on your wild excursions decade after decade. And all I have to show for it is pain—no, embarrassment."

The wizard spoke in a stern tone to his floating ingredients. They froze midair, and the cauldron's bubbling dulled to a soft roar. He lowered his spectacles and sized up Barath with his wand hand. His branches were bare except for bits of torn bark and cracking pit marks.

"I apologize, my loyal companion. My quest to create the stones and bring back the dragons is dire, but I've neglected something of immense value—friendship." Letting his brewing cauldron rest for a moment, the potion wizard spun his hand in tight circles and chanted to his wand, "Ehm-eease, meh-heease...branches are bare and cold. The warmth from leaves, magic if you please."

In seconds, Barath sprouted vivid red, flowery leaves. They were fluffy and thick, covering his branches.

"Whoa!" Sterling said, taken aback by the transformation.

"Well...I suppose no one will guess I'm a tree—more of a stumpy barrel of redbird fluff," Barath said, sounding defeated.

*He does look a little silly.* Sterling held back a smirk, careful not to insult the tiny tree. "Are those...real leaves, sir? I've never seen anything like them before."

"They are a simulation of real leaves. This kind grows on a tropical island I'm particularly fond of—but that doesn't matter. Barath, you will be warm. Now, back to our stone! The dark spell on our dragons grows stronger with each passing moment!"

"Can the stones really bring the dragons back?

What happens if he doesn't make them fast enough?" Sterling asked Barath.

The grumpy tree gave him the silent treatment— that, or he was too preoccupied with combing his bright new leaves.

The wizard flurried his wand hand, continuing his work on the potion but he'd heard the question. "The stones are complicated, but if we don't hurry, the dragons will be gone from our realm—maybe forever. Jeanno has become more dangerous with the dragons no longer in Everen. You see, he plans to become the most powerful magic doer in Everen at any cost. Worst of all, he will siphon magic from every creature with a drop in it—take it all for himself and his Ottomon Wizard fanatics."

"What's the point of all that magic? What does he want with it?" Sterling pried.

"Immortality, boy!" the wizard said as if it were the only obvious answer. "Haven't you learned what your witches were after? Darkness does not want to die—it craves eternal existence. It steals life from anywhere or anyone that it can. What has your Alin taught you, anyhow?"

"It's not his fault. I didn't listen—and I didn't ask," Sterling lied. He was embarrassed that Tomorak wouldn't let him borrow his books about magic creatures, let alone teach him important magical history. No, he had to sneak the Alin's books from his library like an untrustworthy child.

"Well, you certainly have a flow of questions for

me!" the wizard remarked. "Boy, why do you think Alins are so few these days? There used to be towers of them—the Vionin Kingdom housed thousands. Now, there's scarcely enough to assign one to each village. Who do you think was responsible for their disappearance?"

The answer hit him like a metal pot over the head, and memories of dark wizard tales erupted inside his mind.

*They trick innocent creatures and kidnap children in the moonlight. They are the dreadful moans in the forest at night, the watchers through bedroom windows that send tingles up your spine. They move in the shadows, searching for lives to take.*

"The Ottomon Wizards attacked them, didn't they? Jeanno wanted the Alins gone—they were too powerful," Sterling said, shaking his head. His face went pale as he accepted that another childhood tale was more than that.

The potion wizard nodded and unlocked the sphere of glowing White Mountain snow. "You *are* a fast learner—that will come in handy." Sterling rolled his eyes at the backhanded compliment, but the wizard continued, "Now, let's finish this potion. An ingredient as rare as this one must be carefully sifted to a precise amount. Too much and the potion will freeze. Too little and the spell will not take. Do you know how it's measured?"

Sterling twitched his eyebrows and tried to stay focused on the conversation. "I don't suppose ordinary food scales would work. Considering you're a wizard, a magic scale or something that makes loud noises or fire," he said honestly.

"Wizards do enjoy fire. But no. The most accurate scale cannot be bought or even conjured."

Sterling shrugged his shoulders. "Beats the Everen outta me, sir."

The potion wizard grinned. "It must come freely from a dragon. As it happens, centuries ago when I was a young warlock, a brave wizard fought alongside a pack of stone dragons in battle but suffered a fatal wound. On his deathbed, a stone dragon princess gave one of her scales to cure the wizard. He lived to tell the tale, and he passed the scale to me when the time was right."

The potion wizard wiped magic drippings from a silver dragon scale, sturdy and metallic. Its smooth surface shone brightly.

"Because he knew you'd become a potion maker and would need it?" Sterling guessed.

"Ah, that story is for another time, hunter boy," the potion wizard whispered with a wink. His scraggly eyebrows wiggled a bit before stretching back into place.

As methodically as Sterling's father cleaning his hunting ax, the potion wizard locked the silvery scale into position over a barrel of pale blue liquid. Then, a handful of mountain snow sparkled as it slid from a crystal-lined pouch onto the scale. The snow wobbled, nearly tipping down the smooth edges and onto the moist cave floor. It rolled to the peak of the scale and spun into a perfect sphere.

"It's time," said the wizard.

A golden leaf slid beneath the glowing sphere and lowered it (slowly) into the cauldron. The mixture hissed and bubbled before it sloshed into a hurricane spiral. Then, like the glass stone, the potion transformed entirely into something else.

The second stone appeared in the glow of purple crystals gleaming from the arched ceiling. The stone was gray with swirls of deep purple strands, and a white light sparkled inside. Sterling's eyes were glued to the shimmery object—magnificent and no less impressive than the first stone.

"By name, it is called 'the Mountain Stone' but known more often as 'Mountain's Breath' by magic doers," the potion wizard explained. "It contains the beauty and danger of the snowy mountain peaks themselves."

From the corners of the cave, the seven sisters spoke.

"The Mountain Stone of strength has been reborn. Five more stones remain. Your skill is impressive, Potion Wizard, but the tasks ahead bring challenges you have not faced. It is wise to have the hunter with you—he is a flame against the darkness. Together, your destiny leads to the chosen one—a child. He is the key to the rest of your story and to ours..." The voices trailed off.

"A child?" The potion wizard was befuddled.

Sterling hadn't known the wizard for more than a few days, but he could tell when silence was best. Crystal chips smoldered, and the cave felt more like home somehow. He sat next to the wizard's purple fire (it wasn't as warm as he had hoped) and sharpened his dagger with a special stone his father had given him.

"This wasn't part of my plan—I intend to conjure the most powerful potions to fight the darkest wizard of our time. It is too treacherous for an ordinary child unless..." He scratched his bearded chin then perked up as if he had figured out a riddle. "Well, this is most unexpected. If I am right, my young witch hunter, I believe you will very much wish to meet this child." He cocked his head to the side and puffed on his pipe.

Sterling couldn't deny it. This journey, the disappearance of the dragons, the potions, the dark wizards, and the seven sisters—it called to him despite the danger of it all. The wizard was right. He wanted more than anything to meet the chosen one, whatever consequences it would bring.

## CHAPTER THIRTEEN
# THE FIRE PLANT

The tops of volcanoes, while wondrously wild, were about the last sight Sterling wanted to see up close. Fire Dragons would've been the only thing worse. Even those winged, fire-breathing monsters stayed away from the enormous heat stacks. Maybe these had once been peaceful mountains that had made a deal with the devil. They went dormant for years but would spew lava and black ash without notice. Volcanoes never died—*Don't trust something that doesn't die*, Sir Rider Fierce had warned.

"How did this wizard talk us into flying over volcanoes? That's easy. He didn't mention the volcanoes. Did he, Banefield? It's enough to make me want to just go home." Sterling patted his horse's neck, but Banefield snorted and kept flying right behind the potion wizard. After all, this wasn't a good place to lose one's way.

They circled one of the prominent volcanoes for what felt like an eternity. The leather saddle started to overheat and smell like roasted fur. Soon, Sterling felt like he'd gotten a nasty sunburn on his backside, and whiffs of horse sweat grew more pungent.

The potion wizard seemed to be in no rush. Instead, he meticulously measured the volcanoes with a gold gadget that gleamed as bright as a star. The brightness was a good thing because it was the only reason Sterling could follow the wizard through billowing black air without getting lost. The potion wizard was a fast flyer, even with Barath (and his new bright red leaves) clinging to his back.

*Barath looks like a wooden backpack full of ripe red apples, but I'm not going to be the one to tell him.*

The wizard darted into a clearing, and Banefield dove after him. They caught up to the potion wizard and flew alongside him. The wizard's beard fluttered in the smoldering air, charred in places. Bits of his cap and robe bore tiny holes, a telltale sign of lava spray.

"The fire plant! I've found it! Wizard's luck, I tell you. The fire finder works like a charm! Aunt Edmonstone would be proud! This glittery gadget teased me from atop her enchanted shelves for eighty years before she parted with it. She said it was mine forever if I'd promised to use it—pizzah, I've done it!" The potion wizard held up the golden instrument to match the volcano notches. It lined up with the mountainous terrain perfectly.

Barath sighed. "I'm not fond of molten innards

and scalding volcanic rock, no matter the prize. We'll be charred meals for the volcano lizards if we don't take our leave soon." He shook his branches—some leaves detached, falling like red snow flurries.

Sterling wished for snow—a blizzard. Even the snow leopard howls would be welcome if it meant he could cool down. Anything was better than feeling like his insides were being roasted.

Suddenly, Barath turned around.

"The hunter boy and his horse smell worse than troll sweat. They shouldn't be here," Barath said in a matter-of-fact tone.

"It's not like I asked," Sterling retorted before he could stop himself. "And stop calling me 'boy.'"

One of the more prominent fire mountains nearby released hot gas, and lava soared above them like rain.

"Hurry, hunter! Come close!" the potion wizard commanded. He conjured an ice bubble large enough for them all to squeeze inside.

Sterling hugged his horse and galloped straight for it. He shut his eyes until he heard a familiar voice.

"You're safe for now. The ice magic wouldn't last long, I'm afraid—not here," the potion wizard warned.

"Thank you," Sterling replied. "Easy now," he whispered to Banefield, wiping soot from the horse's neck. Instead, it smeared black gunk into his soft, wet coat. Banefield neighed gratefully.

The ice walls were thicker than any house wall—they resembled cave rock, only smoother. Sterling pushed his face against the ice, and immediately, his skin thanked him. The magical ice sphere began melting, but the ice droplets felt like heaven on his forehead and shoulders. Besides, he didn't like to complain. He was a hunter—it wasn't in his nature.

"And what is your plan now that we're about to be roasted in flames?" Barath whined.

"Hang on—hang on tight is the plan!" the potion wizard shouted. He waved his arms, and the ice bubble lifted off the ground. It sped through the air, diving toward the center of a volcano as Sterling positioned Banefield in the center of the bubble where the floor was flattest.

They plummeted downward through puffs of pitch-black smoke, stopping just before crashing into the volcano's mouth. The potion wizard muttered an ancient spell in a language only other wizards or Barath could have understood. A portal hole appeared, allowing him to transport himself outside without cracking the ice bubble. Inside, Sterling, Banefield, and Barath waited under icy drips that soon melted into a lukewarm puddle.

"How long should he be gone?" Sterling asked. He peered through the magical ice wall and caught a glimpse of the wizard's cap.

"Not long. After using up most of his magic energy on flying enchantments for your horse, and now this ice ball, he'll be zapped," Barath explained.

"Zapped?"

"Don't you know anything about wizards? His

magic levels will fall too low for him to recharge on his own."

Sterling watched as the wizard floated over oozing streaks of bright orange lava. The volcano was raven black, and the cracks reminded him of a bread dough cracking in the oven. The potion wizard bent near a patch of fire, and his spindly fingers snatched a bit of flame. He'd conjured himself back inside the (now very melted) ice ball in a flash.

"I've got it! The rare and enchanting—" the potion wizard began.

"Time's running out! My leaves are charring. Can we leave this wretched death sauna now?" begged Barath.

"Patience!" said the potion wizard with a grin. His wand glowed electric blue, and he curled his fingers in circles. Tiny pearl beads danced from the wand toward the fire plant, luring the purest fire leaves from its stem. Fire and ice swirled in an infinity pattern, and one perfect fire leaf appeared inside a small ice sphere.

"The fire leaf is now cool enough for safekeeping on our journey home but hot enough not to die out. Precision is a delicate art," the potion wizard stated proudly, wiping sparkling sweat from his brow.

"Sir, this is brilliant—but, uh, the volcano seems, I don't know, sort of angry that you took its plant," Sterling noted as the volcano rumbled.

The ice bubble began to shake. It toppled downward and crashed into a rock. It began rolling down the volcano, losing chunks of precious ice with each crash against the scalding mountain. Barath dug his branches into the ice walls, but poor Banefield's hooves slipped against the wet surface. They rolled faster and bounced high into the air before dropping back toward the base of the volcano. Sterling dove beneath his horse, determined to try to protect him.

"You'll be crushed, hunter boy!" Barath exclaimed in a tone that scared Sterling to his core. He knew that he was right.

## CHAPTER FOURTEEN
# THE RUMBLE OF A DRAGON

"This is what friends do," Sterling gasped with outstretched hands. He'd used his "hunter's sight" to aim, hurling himself at the ice where Banefield's head would impact.

His vision went dark. He fumbled to touch his ribs and legs. They were in the right places and didn't feel broken. His head throbbed, and he had no sense of the ice ball's whereabouts or whether they were still rolling down the volcano. Had it not been for the potion wizard casting a protection cloak around him sometime during the fall, the weight of the horse would have indeed crushed his body.

"Nothing broken. How about you, boy?" Sterling asked Banefield, patting the horse's neck.

Banefield snuffled softly. Thankfully, he was uninjured. Sterling's vision returned blurry but effective. They sat in a mess of ice chunks, all that remained of the ice ball.

Barath sputtered words that must've been native meute curse words, but his fluffy red leaves were mostly intact.

The potion wizard released a slight cackle and shuffled aside chunks of ice to uncover his wand. "We made it to the bottom. You didn't think I'd let harm come to either of you?"

Sterling smiled and remembered the first time his father had taken him hunting. He'd slipped over a mossy tree trunk into a river, and his father had shot an arrow into the trunk for Sterling to hold. He didn't get washed down the river but instead used the arrow to pull himself from the current. It was comforting to have someone look out for him the way his father had, even if it was a quirky old wizard. Still, Sterling couldn't help but wonder why the wizard had brought him along if he only needed to be saved over and over.

Then, something thundered nearby.

"The volcano's going to blow!" Barath screeched, clenching his wooden teeth together.

The potion wizard perked up, but instead of being alarmed, he smiled.

"Oh, Barath, you desperately need to tune your magic finder. The rumbling isn't our scorching volcano, though she's displeased I took a prized fire plant from her collection," said the wizard.

*Rumble. Rumble.*

"Sir—there is something coming. Something big," Sterling whispered. His hunter's hearing never failed.

"Yes, yes. Brace yourself, my young hunter. We're about to have company."

Sterling nodded in understanding, and his hand reflexively went to his dagger. He didn't sense a witch, but whatever was coming, it was his duty to stand guard.

Through clouds of ash, a giant green dragon stumbled toward them. His talons slipped on the black surface, and he fell, making a terrible boom. His knees and tail were painted with soot stains from a series of falls, and the stars on his once purple vest were barely visible through the muck.

"This can't be. All the dragons are gone!" exclaimed Barath.

"I can't see very well. Who's there? Oh, I see you now—wow, a talking plant!" The dragon's voice was high-pitched and full of childish curiosity. Sterling's brow furrowed. He'd been brought along to protect the wizard from this?

"Plant? Hah! I'm no more a plant than you are an oversized lizard."

The potion wizard straightened his cap extra pointy and smiled as graciously as a host welcoming friends to a dinner party. "Barath, you're not being kind to our new friend. Most have never heard of, let alone seen, a meute such as yourself. Dragon child, this is Barath of Latos, a magical and grumpy miniature tree. I suppose living to be ancient and wise doesn't mean he has to obtain manners," he chuckled. "And I am—"

"I know who you are. You're Thahn, the greatest potion wizard of our time—maybe of any time." The dragon squeaked out his words in a hurry.

Sterling detected fear in the dragon boy's words, but his hunter's instincts alerted him to the dangerous parts of the dragon. The emerald-green behemoth was equipped with a mouthful of razor-sharp teeth that could snap a witch hunter in half and chomp Banefield to horse dust. Even the dragon's tail was a weapon, tipped with jagged scales and powerful enough to knock over a house.

*I can't trust this creature. Even a dragon child is a serious threat.*

The potion wizard finished rattling off introductions, which didn't seem to calm the dragon.

"My name is Green and I've come to find you. Something has happened to my family—to my village —to all dragons. They've all disappeared! I know it sounds impossible, but it's true. There's a book about a potion wizard—you helped dragons before. Please, help me bring them back. I think you're the only one who can," the dragon child said with a forced smile (full of sharp, yellow teeth) and glints of emerald shining from his eyes.

"Ah-ha! You're a Story Dragon! I wasn't sure your kind existed outside of folklore and wild imaginations anymore. Yet here you stand. This is a most exciting day. Right, Barath?"

"Bah, I say!" The meute shook his branches, and

piles of blackened leaves fell to the ground, burned to a crisp from their earlier volcano dealings.

"My dear hunter—I'd bet all the magic in my little pinky (which is a fair amount) that you've never met a dragon before," said the wizard, smiling gleefully.

Sterling nodded in silence. He didn't want to talk about when his friend Gahbe had been practically roasted to death in dragon fire in the Eastlands. If it hadn't been for the Red Wolf, a giant in his own right, the Fire Dragons would've cooked and eaten Gahbe whole.

Green stood and stared at all the commotion, unsure what to make of it all. Sterling was uneasy. Banefield stomped as his hooves smoldered in volcanic soil. Barath started cursing in a meute dialect again. The potion wizard was the only one remotely pleased.

"I hope I'm not being rude, but can you help me or not? I've come all this way to find you." Green sniffed back tears. When he turned toward Sterling, his eyes had shifted to a yellowish brown instead of the vibrant emerald from a moment ago. His words were like that of a seven- or eight-year-old human child.

The potion wizard whizzed his wand around. Barath's crisped leaves settled into a neat pile as the soot floated off his branches. Next, a cooling mist slipped beneath Banefield's hooves. Finally, a globby purple swirl rolled along the dragon, cleaning char marks from his paws, knees, and plump tail.

"Green the Story Dragon, I will help you find your

parents. In fact, I intend to find all the dragons," the potion wizard boomed. "We'll go to my cave. I will show you what I've been working on. But that's only part of the plan. You are the key to breaking the dragons' curse."

Green thought hard, like he was stumped on a math test meant for much older dragons.

"Um, thank you, but I should tell you that I can't fly or breathe wind or fire or anything—I'm not much of a real dragon. I'm sorry. I-I don't know how I can help," he confessed.

"The spell did not work on you, Story Dragon. You have unique abilities—you are a dragon—a very rare kind," the potion wizard said softly as he concocted a magic cloud of dust.

A volcano hissed, then boomed in the distance.

"It's time to go. Are you coming along or are you going to hang around these pesky volcanoes?" the potion wizard asked with a chuckle.

Green waited and watched the odd group step inside a floating dust sphere. He hesitated, then leaped inside, straining its edges and still managing to crowd the horse. And away they flew.

# CHAPTER FIFTEEN
## AN EMERALD FLAME

The wizard brewed a large batch of potion that evening, cloaked in the safety of his cave. Fat squatty bottles and squiggly slender ones scooted through the air at his command. Sterling and Green stared wide-eyed at the dancing ingredients while Barath napped; Sterling was quickly learning that trees slept a lot. But he figured Banefield was also dozing outside the cave with a belly full of oats and honey grass the wizard had conjured for him. The return flight from the Eastlands was uneventful but took a heavier toll on the travelers due to the strong headwinds.

Colorful liquids sloshed about, and the occasional puff of powder erupted from the ancient cauldron. Some lumpy goo poured in drop by drop, each splash changing the brew's color. It went from magenta to black, then mustard yellow to rocky red.

"I've never met a potion wizard before," Green

whispered, full of excitement. "Do you think he can do what he says? Create the seven stones—bring back the seven sisters to break the spell on the dragons?"

Sterling smiled and relaxed his shoulders, thankful that the dragon couldn't breathe fire or do anything traditionally dragon-like. It was safer that way.

"He's already made two of the stones. This is his third," Sterling said in his best big-brother type of voice. "You'll see."

"The bottles look like medicine jars from Mother's cabinet. But ours are made with thick glass and coated with dust. Mother only pulls them out if I get sick or hurt," Green recalled.

"I hadn't considered that dragons had a need for medicine," said Sterling.

"Oh yes, and she had a bottle for every color of the rainbow—and any homemade cure a dragon might need. A sour belly got a pink bottle, headaches were a bright yellow bottle, and there was a fizzy brown one for pain that tickled my tongue—tasted terrible!"

Sterling studied the enormous green dragon sitting within arm's reach. His scales rested one upon the other to create a smooth surface that clicked into place like stone puzzle pieces when he moved. His tail encircled his body like a blanket around a cozy child.

Sterling tried to sound reassuring. "We'll do whatever it takes to get your family back, even if I have to face the dark wizards myself."

"Thank you, Sterling Fierce," said Green.

"You can just call me Sterling."

Suddenly, the cauldron spewed and spat over its stained edges. The potion wizard raised his arms and turned toward the witch hunter and the dragon child.

"Come stand by the cauldron—quickly! My dear Story Dragon, hold this fire leaf firmly in one claw."

Green approached the potion, but his tail quivered.

"You'll be fine. Dragons have an incredible ability to withstand hot temperatures," Sterling whispered.

"Here," the wizard said as he released a fire leaf from its protective sphere. It floated in the air, and its flame doubled in size.

Green stretched out his palm, and the fire leaf settled in it. He tiptoed to the lively brew.

"Now what?"

"Carefully drop it in, then stand back," whispered the wizard.

Green did as he was told.

As the flaming plant touched the potion, it coiled into a black flame and sank to the bottom of the liquid goop.

*Glop. Blop.*

"Try once more," the potion wizard instructed with an encouraging smile, releasing another fiery leaf.

It charred and shriveled like a black raisin. The potion wizard paced back and forth. His whispers were in an ancient wizard language, and his beard hairs braided and unbraided themselves hurriedly.

"There's only one leaf left now. See...I'm not special after all," Green sulked.

Sterling chewed his lip. His mind raced. "Maybe you need to say a charm or magic spell or something?"

"Ah, Everen's fairies and all the Azcar berries in the King's castle, I've got it! Hold the last fire leaf close to you—look at it closely. What do you see?" The potion wizard panted.

Green stared into the fire leaf.

"Nothing. Just fire," the dragon said in his saddest voice. Then his eyes grew wide.

"Wait—there's something! It's a ring of planets— seven of them!" The fire leaf sparked a bright green flame right before their eyes.

"Green fire?!" he exclaimed with a toothy grin, his eyes sparking bright green again. "It's ready to go in now. I don't know how I know, but I do."

The potion wizard nodded in approval.

The emerald flame danced in Green's eyes as he released the leaf into the cauldron. Bubbles gurgled, and bits of rock spewed out. The green fire leaf spun a tight twirl in the air. Then, it dove deep into the heart of the brew. The potion swirled into a tiny hurricane, thrashing with great speed. A rainbow cyclone flashed with a beam of cold white light that stretched to the cave's ceiling. Purple crystals shattered above.

"Take cover!" Barath hollered, disappearing into his wall nook for safety.

Crystals poured from the cave's ceiling like angry

purple rain. The wizard spouted a spell in wizard speak, creating an umbrella-shaped mist. Sterling tugged Green beneath it as the crystal shards crashed down in a roar.

After a minute, the sounds of breaking crystal quieted, and Sterling squinted around the cave. The purple dust had settled, covering the entire potion lab.

"Would it hurt you to warn anyone when you do that?" Barath grumped between coughs. "Wizards! This sense of adventure is dangerous. I'll never understand why simple safety precautions can't be part of the plan. Thank the stars for wizard's luck or I'd have no branches left. And this after those atrocious volcanoes!"

The potion wizard laughed from his belly and beamed. "Green, my boy! Do you see what you've done? You were the missing ingredient, can't you see? No one could have turned that fire green—except for a Story Dragon. You are pure magic from head to tail!"

"Let's not get carried away," Barath interrupted. "He's only a boy, after all. We've all had enough commotion for one day. I know I have." Crystal dust trickled from his branches, and he wiped his trunk with blackened leaves (they still looked pitiful after the volcano encounter). Lava soot scraped into his bark, and he whimpered.

"The volcanoes did as volcanoes are meant to do, my companion. It is us out of place and invading their homeland. And you were wrong on one last account —they were marvelous!"

With a swish of the wizard's wand, tiny streaks of glowing lights rushed toward the grumpy meute. New leaves sprouted, filling his branches with feather-like wisps, long and silky.

Barath hugged his new leaves and swayed back and forth. "I suppose you must feel guilty. These are a handsome lot of leaves," he squealed in what sounded almost like happiness.

"As long as it keeps you quiet for a time. Now, what say you, dragon?" asked the potion wizard.

Green smiled. "I am not sure. Did it work?"

The potion wizard held up his finger and motioned for Green to investigate the cauldron. Inside was a clear stone filled with flickering flames of red and green.

"This is the Fire Stone. Though there's been debate over its name over the ages—fire, lava; some call it the devil's stone, but I won't hear any of that nonsense. Now, together, we can make the other four."

"What do we do after the stones are made?" Sterling asked.

"Once the stones are made, the sisters will have strength to help us," he said placidly. "Jeanno's curse is strong, but Story Dragon magic is unique—ancient and very powerful. With Green's magic, we can bring back the power of the seven sisters. Together, we can counteract Jeanno's spell and make sure he'll never threaten them again." The potion wizard spoke as calmly as if he were explaining the steps to make bread dough.

Sterling had stayed mostly quiet during all the fireworks, and he'd tried to believe in Thahn's plan. But secretly, he couldn't help but wonder if it would be better to get in touch with the Ottomon clan—to talk to Jeanno and try to strike a deal. Even a mad wizard might want something else to trade for the dragons. Most magical creatures were open to trades. In fact, they seemed to enjoy the whole bargaining process—that and riddles.

*Probably something to do with entertaining themselves in their long lives*, he thought. Besides, what did the wizard mean by "never again"? Didn't the dark wizards deserve the chance to resolve things peacefully? Sterling's brooding silence was interrupted by an uncertain sigh.

Green stared at the stone; his face scrunched up in puzzlement. Sterling sensed the young dragon was doubting both himself and the wizard. How could he trust this wizard when another wizard had cursed dragons in the first place?

*Maybe the Story Dragon could be convinced to fight with me, especially if he's as powerful as the potion wizard claims.*

Almost as if he'd heard Sterling's thoughts, Green sighed and said, "What if my dragon magic isn't enough?"

"I'll prove it to you now—you have the power to fix what has been broken," the potion wizard touted.

Green tilted his head in confusion and turned to Sterling, who shrugged. "His plan does seem a little crazy, but if it works, it's worth a try. And you can tell he's a good wizard. He's not just good at magic, he's the good kind of magic doer—trust me. I've met the ones who aren't," Sterling said, rubbing his forearms where his witch-killing blood swam.

Green nodded. "Okay. What do I need to do?"

"First, you must believe you can do extraordinary things," the potion wizard said. He whooshed his wand around, and brilliant red-and-green flashes of fire danced inside the stone. It floated into a decorative box where the other two stones were secured.

"Tell me, how did you know to find our witch hunter and me at the base of a desolate volcano in the middle of the all-but-abandoned Eastlands?"

Green swallowed and gulped out one word: "Magic."

# CHAPTER SIXTEEN
# THE GROBBENSES' TOWER

S terling had coughed up a fair amount of volcanic soot after returning from the Eastlands, but that hadn't helped combat the fatigue he felt. For once, the cave was not too cold. In fact, it was the perfect temperature for sleeping. The potion wizard immediately set about planning his next recipe, but Green curled up in a dry patch and was soon snoring dragon-size snores. Sterling settled just out of reach of the dragon's wafting breaths and kicking feet and peered at the stones they'd risked so much to concoct.

*Maybe I can take a tiny rest—a meute-sized nap.*

The second Sterling's eyelids closed, he felt his body descend like he'd fallen into a bottomless pit. He'd begun his first hunter's sight—yet another of his father's stories that had more truth to it than Sterling had realized. He was out of his body, floating in red liquid like he was swimming underneath a crimson sea. He could breathe, which helped lessen his panic. The sound of his own heartbeat filled the murky gel, vibrating in his ears until a light appeared.

It was an image—a standing figure emerged through what looked like a porthole clouded by red-tinted mist. Sterling concentrated harder, pushing his hunter vision ability to its max.

Eventually, the image zoomed closer until he could see a figure. A mop of black hair, tightly curled, sprang up and down, gleaming with mineral oil and sea silk. Spindly locks shook vigorously as this figure paced a laboratory in a circular room. Tables were covered in gleaming brass gadgets, and the sun was setting over the Northern Sea outside the window.

Hazy words drifted to Sterling.

"Don't you worry. Those dragons won't be harming anyone ever again. I'll make sure of it."

"No, Jeanno, don't let them kill any more families like they did mine."

Sterling tried to catch a glimpse of the other person in the wizard's tower, but just then, something grabbed his foot. Sterling yelped and looked down.

At first, he saw nothing unusual, but then the vision ended and his eyes snapped open. A huge green dragon mouth was clamped onto Sterling's boot.

"Green!"

Sterling wiggled his foot, but the jaws were locked tight. Yet it didn't hurt. Sterling shoved at the young dragon, and eventually, Green let go with a snort. Sterling scooted farther away and closed his eyes, trying to recapture the hunter's vision, but instead, he drifted off into a more normal nap.

For the next few days, the group of unlikely companions traveled east, then north, until they reached the Northern Ice Lands. Sterling trailed Green, who followed the potion wizard, who occasionally swept them up in a flying spell but usually let them walk. From time to time, Barath mumbled about being uncomfortable on the potion wizard's shoulder, but even Thahn ignored him. Finally, they arrived at a rugged mountain landscape, expansive and blanketed with a powdery frost. Hours passed as they trekked through valleys and spiraled their way around the mountains.

"Where are we?" Sterling broke the silence. The cold air made his lungs feel heavy, and he started wishing he was in the volcano lands instead.

"Dangling on the slippery strip of an icy stairway spiraling up an abandoned Grobbenses' Tower, that's where," Barath muttered—shoving words into the freezing air and then snapping his wooden lips closed.

"What is a G-Grobbens?" Green squeaked.

Grobbenses were extinct. Sterling knew this, but it didn't stop the prickling from spreading inside his stomach as they approached the top of the tower.

Sterling spit out some hunter knowledge, pushing through the cold in his chest. "Grobbenses were a nasty bunch. Sharp teeth and bald heads. They attacked for any reason."

"Have you seen a Grobbens before?" asked Green in a shaky voice.

Sterling couldn't see Green, but he imagined the dragon's beautiful green eyes were dull, which seemed to happen when he was sad or scared.

Barath chimed in, "Loathsome creatures, Grobbenses—the hunter boy is correct. None are friendly. They are savage even to their own kind. Murderous troll-beasts and thieves."

The potion wizard hooted from higher up the staircase. "Yes, yes. Grobbenses have been this way for centuries—runs deep in their blood." He was several spirals ahead of them, using his staff for balance.

Green paused in his tracks. "They, um. They're not here anymore?"

Sterling tilted his head at the tower and ran his hand along its icy stone walls. "How could something wicked build a tower like this? It's magnificent. The detail in the sculpting is almost, well, joyful."

"If you're asking if any Grobbenses could conceive of returning to reclaim this tower, you needn't worry, my friends. They all but perished from Everen some time ago. They were not always hideous and violent. On the contrary, they were once peaceful, small, and plump creatures—good workers and pleasant."

"Here comes the history lesson," said Barath with a moan.

"Their leaders, the Sethst Family, were obsessed with finding treasure. Once, they were after jewels of the ancient Analla civilization that had been lost at sea and were said to be especially valuable. There had been a shipwreck, and the entire crew of Analla drowned. Their precious jewels sank below, buried deep beneath the salty waters, cursed by the Anallas' death. Nobody knew how the Grobbenses came to possess a map to the jewels, but they dug long enough and deep enough. Finally, they found the lost Anallan jewels.

"Slowly, the Sethst Family went mad, then all the Grobbenses. They feared others would steal the jewels, so they dug holes in the earth, burying themselves with their precious sea jewels."

"So, the jewels were cursed by the sea or by the Anallas?" Sterling asked.

Green piped up, "Who'd want to live underground anyway?"

"The point is that greed can rot the mind entirely to madness," the wizard explained.

He neared the top steps of the tower. "Their appearance decayed along with their poisoned hearts and minds. Razor-sharp teeth and hairless heads were a frightful sight. A few Grobbenses may yet live, but their hearts would be too weak to keep them in anything but a state of hibernation—a deep and painful sleep. They won't part with their treasure, cursed along with it beneath the ground in the company of mud beetles and eyeless worms."

The potion wizard ended his story like he'd told an ordinary history lesson. He puffed a pipe calmly and watched white wafts of smoke toss and turn through the air. The burning orange bits landed on the icy stairs with a hiss.

"Did anyone try to save them? The Grobbenses, I mean?" Green inquired.

"Can't help those who don't want it," Barath harrumphed. "Thahn, our talented potion wizard here, tried it a long time ago. They clawed up his wizard's staff and nearly shredded my trunk to splinters. I'd give my top branch if I never had to come across a Grobbens again," admitted Barath.

He revealed five long marks along his trunk.

"Those look like claws—or teeth marks," Sterling noted.

"Right you are, hunter boy. This is where the jewel thieves dragged their teeth into me. We got too close to their treasure," said Barath.

"Lucky to've escaped that one ol' boy? I wasn't as wise then—I thought they could be saved. But no wizards' magic could break the curse once their hearts were infected," the potion wizard said.

Barath itched his trunk scars and surveyed the tower's entrance with caution.

They had reached the top of the stairs and were standing before the grand entrance. The doors were stone and covered in a thick layer of ice. The wind howled, and an eerie cracking sound fidgeted in the distance.

"If we do see a Grobbens, fire is the only weapon that'll work," Sterling said to Green. "I read that in a book, I think."

The potion wizard nodded. "Good idea, witch hunter! Fire! We can melt the ice from these doors. Story Dragon, can you summon your fire—the green flame?"

"I-I'm not sure. I don't have fire magic. It was just the fire leaf that made it earlier," Green stuttered.

The potion wizard gazed into the distance, deep into the mountains surrounding the tower. "I shouldn't be the one to teach you, but since your parents can't be and they are the ones that need saving, here it goes." He turned back to Green. "Magic lesson number one. Concentrate on your back scales, where your shoulders come together."

Green didn't argue. If anyone wanted to keep away Grobbenses, he did.

"Now, pick up that dead tree branch. Run it across your scales. Think only of green fire in your mind. See it form into a shape. Feel the flame's heat. Tell it what to look like—it will listen to you," the potion wizard declared.

Green tried, but all he could think about was a bald, squatty pale creature with shark teeth coming at him.

"Green, I believe you can do it," Sterling whispered.

Green smiled at the kind words. He closed his eyes and concentrated harder than when he'd tried to breathe wind gusts or fly like the other dragons.

Suddenly, a ball of green fire flickered peacefully in the air like a hot, gleaming emerald. Sterling helped

Green nudge the fireball toward the tower entrance, melting the ice from its meticulously sculpted doors. Once the locks were exposed, the potion wizard whispered an enchantment as his wand bobbed in his hand. The rusted bolts slammed aside into an unlocked position. Heavy stone slabs made a dreadful creak as if they were in pain. Finally, metal clasps unlatched one by one, and the Grobbenses' Tower doors opened.

# CHAPTER SEVENTEEN

# SCATTERED FOOTPRINTS

S tepping inside the Grobbenses' Tower felt like stepping back in time. Creaking wood floors and cobwebs on furniture embodied the classic haunted castle described in many children's stories. Sterling squatted to peer through the windows (they were built waist-high for a human but the perfect height for a Grobbens). The tower stood inside a ring of mountains called the Cloud Mountains. Each window presented a beautiful view of the frosty landscape. The Northern Ice Lands were painted in ice, true to their name, and the mountain peaks swirled with white mist. The Grobbenses had settled high in their perch, isolated from much of Everen. From the mountaintops, a river flowed, full of rare bluegills, an elusive but tasty cold-water fish. Despite frozen banks, the current rippled downward. The land was silent except for trickling water that only a hunter like Sterling could hear from this distance.

He understood how this arctic land could be a desirable home from inside the tower. However, the tower itself was another story. The stone walls had faded into a singular coat of gray. Frozen dust covered otherwise cheerful statues. Bearded spiders had left a messy crisscross of webbing over oil paintings, muting their bright colors and textures. Woolly worm tubes spread across smooth, arched ceilings and miniature-sized furniture. Tapestries with torn threading hung above the great hall's dining table. The oval-backed chairs lay flipped over and splintered.

"Well, it's not completely deserted," Sterling said as long-haired ant beds and loose dirt crunched beneath his boots.

"When the Grobbenses left, other creatures, namely insects, claimed the tower as their own. I'm afraid nobody has cared for this place in many years." The potion wizard confirmed what they were all thinking. "It was beautiful in its time—every stone placed in a particular way—very handsome and built to withstand winter's fury. Ah, the details! See here? It's a season's clock carved inside the wall to mark if the year would bring an ordinary winter or a long winter."

"You've been here before?" Sterling asked. He knew the wizard was old, but it hadn't sunk in how many lifetimes wizards lived and what it must be like to experience so much.

"Yes," he continued without a pause, "and there—a hand-sculpted gown and mitten rack with rotating spindles. It's even plated with copper and gemstones they mined from these very mountains." He let out a yawn and then pulled off his half-moon spectacles. He inspected them and began to wipe off smudges between the folds of his wizard's cape.

"How long have they been gone—the Grobbenses?" asked Green, fumbling with velvet table mats and discarded metal plates.

"I'd say a few hundred years. I'd quite forgotten their tinkering was impressive too! Do you see the engineered pulley system? It's bolted into the cookery to hoist river water inside the tower. It's a shame to see it fall into ruins. I suppose someone could settle here, make repairs, and care for the place again."

"There you go again. Always trying to fix broken things," Barath said as he passed Sterling, Green, and the potion wizard with a huff. Sterling watched as the tiny tree scampered down the tower's interior stairs. They wound tightly with shallow steps perfect for the meute.

"Don't listen to him—he's always grumpy in cold places. We wizards live long lives—most desire to do good in the world. And we seek a purpose for the gifts and time we are given," the potion wizard said, yawning louder. "What does it matter if I like to...fix what I can while I can?"

Suddenly, an unsettling grunt came from below.

Barath barreled back into the room, clasping his new silky leaves. "We are not the only visitors here. Come quick!"

The potion wizard and Sterling ran downstairs, following his gestures. Sterling was light on his feet and arrived first.

"Wizard, sir! Footprints—scattered across the floor. I don't recognize them. These are...unusual," Sterling said, carefully studying the prints without touching them (a good hunter rule).

"Well, it's not Grobbenses, if that's what you're wondering. No. These are not Grobbenses' tracks, but we may wish they were," the potion wizard said. He poked his staff into the hall corner, and straw bits puffed into the air.

"Distinct. Very distinct," the potion wizard mumbled as he retrieved his wand. He cast a pale yellow powder into the sizable pantry where the Grobbenses would've stored their food staples.

Green poked his head around the staircase, sneezing a mixture of dust and dragon boogers.

"I almost got stuck in that little staircase!" He panted. "What did I miss? What did you find?"

"Footprints!" whispered Sterling, not taking his eyes off the wizard.

Barath snorted. "Oh, that's seeker's dust. Whomever he's tracking, there's no escaping seeker's dust!" His wooden smile beamed with pride.

The pale powder fell from the ceiling and clung to

the tracks, outlining them in pale dust. Slowly, a double hourglass shape became visible beside each footprint.

"Over here, big guy." Sterling motioned for Green to keep back from the prints. Large dragon feet would destroy the scene if they weren't careful.

Green fidgeted with his tail, then conjured a small glob of green fire. "Just in case whatever made these prints returns," he said, clutching the flaming fireball.

Barath marched back and forth in the doorway, tapping his branches against the cold stone wall. "What's the verdict, Thahn, my esteemed wizard? My bark senses magical creatures."

Sterling thought aloud, "There were no tracks on the outside stairs—that's the only way in from the ground level—and no prints in the great hall either. They must've come in through the windows."

"Ah, winged creatures! But which ones?" Barath scratched his trunk and concentrated.

Crouching with a looking glass extended from his cap, the potion wizard spoke softly, "It's as I feared. Centipars."

Sterling gasped, and Green nearly gulped down his bright green fire sphere in panic.

"Now, we must remain calm. I'm not altogether certain which pack allegiance it is just yet. It could be any of the factions—possibly just a family trying to stay warm," the potion wizard said, but beads of sweat were forming across his forehead.

"The straw nesting is recent, so they traveled here in cold weather—if that helps," Sterling said.

"Genius, young hunter! That leaves only one possibility." The potion wizard rubbed his hands together and avoided eye contact with the others.

"Well?!" Barath gave an annoyed snort.

"These tracks were made from a small pack of Falcut, the more vicious of the centipars, I'm afraid. The question is not how but why. Why are Falcut in an abandoned tower? It's a guard patrol, four of them. Their job is to protect or to hunt," the potion wizard explained in a hushed tone, sounding more worried than before.

Barath raked his branches across the stone floor. "They're guarding the cloud mist—it's obvious. It's the only thing of value here unless they're digging up zombie Grobbenses to pluck out their cursed sea jewels!"

"I-Isn't that the ingredient we c-came for? Cloud mist?" Green asked, his dragon teeth chattering.

"Someone must've known we'd be coming—they know about the seven stones. Story Dragon, we'll have to move to magic lesson number two and have no time for practice."

Green gnawed his cheek. "It's flying, isn't it?"

He flapped his tiny wings together, looking behind his shoulder. Even Sterling knew they were too small to support the dragon in flight. He shot an encouraging half smile to Green anyway.

"Indeed, my boy. But not flying like a normal dragon," said the potion wizard. "You'll see. Everyone gather around."

## CHAPTER EIGHTEEN
# A CRYSTAL TAIL

"Take a closer look at the prints. The distinct pattern on the floor—right there," the potion wizard said, pointing at a double hourglass shape.

"I couldn't see it before, but the seeking dust—this is incredible! Sir—it's a wing print," Sterling said in excitement.

"Very good, my young hunter. Yes, the Falcut were given a flight enchantment from the Ottomon clan—anyhow, that's their telltale mark and how to track them," the potion wizard said as he weaved a magic sticking spell from Green's back scales to his tail scales. When he was finished, the Story Dragon's plump green tail hung precariously above his head.

"The other dragons didn't look anything like this when they flew. Are you, um, sure this is right?" Green studied his reflection in a metal cup. He could barely stand straight and would've fallen over if he weren't stretching his arms outward to keep balanced.

Barath scooted closer, inspecting the scales. "Oh, you'll fly. But before you know it, your wings will be out of commission—don't get too attached to whatever enchantments you receive. Wizard magic is unpredictable. This is my second new set of leaves this week," he warned, tugging on his silky feather-like leaves.

"You'll do great, Green," Sterling interrupted. "The potion wizard enchanted my horse, and he's flown over Everen just fine." Sterling leaned in, and whispered, "Sure, he's quirky—strange even—but his magic is amazing."

Green swallowed the lump in his throat. "Thank you, Sterling Fierce. I never had a brother, but I hope this is what it feels like."

Sterling nodded. After flying centipars, talking trees, and magic stones, a dragon for a brother wouldn't be that unusual.

The potion wizard pasted another generous helping of magic glue onto Green's tail.

"This will hold your tail bound to your back scales, yes, very good. Now, you're going to fly high enough to take a bit of cloud mist into this ring, then release your tail to let you down."

"I'm not sure I understand. How do I—" But Green was too late to protest.

An electric current zapped from the wizard's spindly fingertips. His hands glowed a majestic purple hue that Sterling had seen only once before in the heart of the Vionin Kingdom (the most magical place in Everen). A puff of bluish fire popped, then smoke spiraled toward the trembling Story Dragon. Suddenly, enormous bubbles sprouted from Green's hind legs. The bubbles stretched and hardened into a gleaming set of crystal wings.

"Wowee!" Green flapped his shiny new wings and soared upward; his emerald eyes widened with pure joy.

"Careful! The stone will shatter them!" Sterling hollered.

Just before Green crashed into the tower ceiling, he flipped over and bounced his large green belly against it.

"Close one—thanks, hunter brother!" Green grinned.

"Easy, dragon! Your new wings are quite breakable —and they won't last long. Now, go out the window. From the tower's top, fly twenty dragon lengths due north until the clouds change into a perfect shade of white. If you're not sure you've gone high enough, tap the ol' nostrils. Your dragon snot should be completely frozen. Only then, open the enchanted ring I gave you. Once the cloud particles are pulled inside the ring, the ring will glow ruby red to signal the job is done. You'll be sure to see it."

"But, what if the wings, you know, run out of magic?" Green flapped the wings and hovered above Sterling. "What if I fall?"

Sterling interjected, "What if you don't?"

Green flashed a dragon smile like a kid on a carousel beaming with joy.

"You got this—big guy!" Sterling couldn't help but smile too. He was genuinely happy to see Green in good spirits.

"Green, my boy, use your tail when the crystal wings disappear. Imagine the glue coming undone— in your mind, see it spring back into place. Swish your tail back and forth and imagine it turning into crystal, just like the crystal wings. You've had the power of flight all along; you just never knew it was in your tail." The potion wizard laughed.

Green clutched the glittering ring on his dragon paw. He took one last glance at his crystal wings, but this time, he was calm.

"I'll be back one way or the other, I suppose," Green said, before bobbing through the large window in the kitchen.

In the Grobbenses' Tower, all became silent. The potion wizard and Barath muddled up the twisted staircase, following a path of crystal wing dust. Sterling eyed the cobweb-drenched ceilings. *There've got to be spiders crawling behind every inch of this place.* Finally, they reached an open archway and spilled out into a perfectly flat, circular tower top.

Sterling inhaled deeper to catch his breath.

"Thin air, boy. Mountain air," Barath commented. "Breathe slow—but not too slow."

The witch hunter nodded and half smiled at the meute.

*I'm taking advice from a tree now.*

They waited. And they waited some more. But their Story Dragon did not return. Soon, the clouds huddled together and became a thick, soupy fog. Sterling began to pace. He had to admit that he'd begun to like Green more than he thought he would. What if something had happened to the young dragon? Barath and the wizard were talking quietly when Sterling whirled on them.

"Shouldn't he be back by now? What if he got lost? What if the centipars found him?"

The potion wizard produced a bejeweled telescope and peered through the clouds.

"I'm sure he's alright..." The potion wizard's voice trailed off.

"But what if he's not? You'd have sent him to his death! I wish you'd sent me with him."

"With him? But what would you have done?"

"What have I been doing the whole time? Why am I even here? I thought it was to protect the last dragon, but even that's pointless if you send him flying away into this soupy mist."

Sterling used his hunter sight, peering into the sky, but the clouds were too thick.

"I should have just stayed in Bren," Sterling muttered. No one replied. He gripped his dagger, wishing he had some enemy to attack or track down. But who was the real enemy here, anyway?

After some time, even Barath scanned the foggy sky. "He's just a child, Thahn. We shouldn't have sent him alone. He doesn't even know how to fly."

But then, a screech echoed from above.

"Yaahoooo!"

Like a page in a children's nursery book, a flying dragon soared through the clouds. His magnificent crystal tail swept back and forth with great force. Tiny gems sparkled like glittering dew.

Green circled his new friends, flying confidently, smiling from ear to ear. He could fly on his own after all.

Sterling felt magic pulsing in the air, rippling in invisible waves over his skin.

The potion wizard beckoned Green to come down. A crash and a roll followed, sending crystal rubble and ice bits everywhere.

The potion wizard laughed from his belly.

"See, my boy? Did you think that oversized tail was good for nothing? It just needed a kickstart. The rest was all your own magic—Story Dragon magic. Might have to work on your landing a bit. That's always the toughest part about flying." The potion wizard squeezed Green in a hug.

Sterling helped shake crystal dust from the dragon's hair tufts while Green snorted with delight. He handed the ring to the potion wizard, and they all gathered around it. A shade of ruby red shone upon their faces. Inside the ring was a teeny bubble that held pure, nearly frozen cloud mist.

"Nowhere else can this ingredient be found. It is rare, but more importantly, powerful," the potion wizard explained, eyeing the ring through half-moon spectacles.

Suddenly, a commotion stirred inside the tower. Metal pots rattled, and the sound of chairs sliding across stone floors told them all they needed to know. Sterling's hand darted to the dagger strapped into his belt.

"Our winged patrol has returned," Barath said, glancing down the tower stairs. His wooden nose twitched.

"Oh no, centipars!" Green whispered as his nostrils flared.

The potion wizard patted Green's tail. "Centipars, yes. A pack of Falcut that you and I won't enjoy meeting. These creatures dislike conversation—they're all teeth and claws if you know what I mean. Let's get your tail in gear for all our sakes."

Just then, dark fur and slick black wings came at them. They flew single file like a sharp, blackened arrow. Green hugged his new friends tightly and put his magic tail to work. In seconds, he lifted the potion wizard, Sterling, and Barath high into the frozen clouds.

*We can vanish into the mist, but the Falcut are excellent trackers*, Sterling worried to himself, looking down at his boots, which dangled in the air. He didn't want to say it out loud; he didn't want Green to lose his concentration, but he knew they wouldn't escape easily.

As if the wizard could hear his thoughts, he nodded at the young witch hunter and winked. "Take us up, Story Dragon, as high as you can, so the ice covers our scent. Falcut can't track what they can't smell." Ice streaks formed over his frumpy leather wizard slippers, and he gripped Barath's trunk snuggly as the Grobbenses Tower faded into a shrinking speck below.

But it was too late for Barath's branches. Silky leaves hardened into pointy feather popsicles, snapping off and plummeting downward like tiny frozen darts. A terrible moaning echoed beneath them, and Sterling's mind went black. Despite the life-threatening cold, Green did as the wizard commanded. He soared even higher.

## CHAPTER NINETEEN
# HEALING CRYSTALS

The flight through the frozen clouds felt like a distant dream, but even in the safety (and warmth) of the cave without a name, Sterling didn't feel like himself. Green was on a roll with fire-making since the Grobbenses Tower, so he made everyone personal-sized campfires to help with thawing out. The emerald-flame creations gave the cave a mystical feel even though the potion wizard was nowhere in sight. He'd rushed out some time ago, muttering in the ancient wizard tongue. He hadn't mentioned when he'd return, but this was how wizards worked—unexpectedly and with purpose, even if no one else could understand.

Sterling was hesitant to trust the potion wizard or any magical being blindly. Thahn had good intentions from all observations, but there had to be something else—other options to help the dragons. Sterling had only met a few witches, but from what he could see, witches and wizards weren't all that similar. In the end, he'd felt like he had to kill the dark witches, but he wondered if things might have been different if there had been more time. Perhaps the dark ones weren't really so evil at heart and just needed the right push to choose what was right. Maybe Jeanno had even banished the dragons by accident! It didn't seem fair to continue with this risky quest without even trying to find a better way. He needed to get Green alone to gauge his opinions about wizards.

Barath bathed in the fire's warmth, drying his bark. Bare branches, scarred from the ice shards, peeked out from the shadows. They were severely damaged, more than before—smaller limbs had snapped under the weight of the ice.

"I'm sorry about your branches, Barath. It's all my fault. I shouldn't have taken us up so high. I—I was afraid the Falcut would catch us. I thought they'd eat us alive," Green said as he warmed his dragon paws by the fire.

Barath shuffled uncomfortably and mumbled something about wizards. He snapped off the rest of his splintered branches.

After a few moments of silence, a tear trickled down Green's cheek. "I wish I could take the flying and the magic back. I don't want magic if it hurts other people—er, things," he sniffed.

"Green, you saved us from the centipars back there. Even the potion wizard couldn't have flown us all at once—not that fast. Having magic is a good thing—and flying too. Maybe you can try a mending spell on Barath's branches?" Sterling suggested.

"Bah. It's not the dragon child's problem to fix. And besides, I've looked a lot worse. Every wizard adventure comes with a price, but I can't leave Thahn. He can be reckless, but he's the only wizard crazy enough to try to save the dragons. Besides, even the most powerful wizards need help sometimes," Barath said.

"The potion wizard needs help?" Green was more confused than ever.

Sterling nodded in agreement with the ancient meute.

"Green, I'll tell you what Sterling Fierce over there probably pieced together by now if he's any good at being a hunter. The centipars will not stop tracking us. Not because they want to eat us, though they might anyway. No. Another wizard sent them. Jeanno will do anything to keep the dragons from returning. Now he knows our potion wizard is trying to bring them back. He knows we're after the seven stones. I've known many wizards, but none as cruel as this one. I'll put it this way, no one with powerful magic is safe around him or his followers. They call themselves the Ottomon Wizards—deranged and deadly folk," Barath said.

"But all the dragons aren't gone; Green's still here," Sterling said. "And the centipars know it."

"You're right, boy. Green, it would be best if you fled, hid away deep inside the mountains where he can't track you..." Barath's voice trailed off as the tall shadow of a wizard filled the entrance of the cave.

"He'll do no such thing! There'll be no nonsense about hiding in mountains and the like. We stay together. My plan will work. I'll keep our Story Dragon perfectly safe!" the potion wizard scolded.

Barath crossed his branches like a pouting child.

Green scurried to the potion wizard. "Wizard! You're bleeding."

A faint oozing of what looked like sky-blue clay spattered the potion wizard's robe. He took rapid, high-pitched breaths (faster than any human could breathe). Then, he collapsed onto the cave floor, sending a puff of crystal dust over their heads. Wisps of purple ash splashed Sterling's cheeks as if someone had sprayed him in the face with cold sand. The wizard chuckled wryly.

"Yes, it seems so. It is time for rest." His next words echoed from every crystal: "Crysteliah pohse hegenia."

Crystal power swirled overhead until the wizard's cap began to glow, then his robe, and finally his worn-out leather slippers. Crystals from the ceiling popped alive, brimming with a deep radiance. The magic was so bright, it lit up the entire cave.

A humming sound pounded in Sterling's ears as he recalled books about magical myths too outlandish to exist. But he was standing next to a dragon, a talking tree, and a wizard. Since leaving the village of Bren (his nonmagical cocoon), he'd seen the real Everen— the wild and magical reality of his homeland. Every make-believe story his father and uncle had told him, even the bad ones, had been true. He instinctively knew what was happening.

In a whirl of purplish light, the potion wizard's body floated to a giant crystal growing at the bottom of the cave.

"I didn't think healing crystals were real," Sterling admitted.

"Oh yes. They are real, and he'll be in there for some time," Barath said with a yawn. A cough barreled out, along with a half dozen splinters.

"Barath, can you heal your branches the same way?" Green asked, a few sharp teeth popping out of his hopeful smile.

"No, the crystals only heal wizards. I require different elements—the forest or the sea. I won't grow any more leaves without nature's help—I'm beyond wizard's magic this time."

"I wish we could help you, Barath," Sterling said.

"Oh, mudbeetles. I've been hurt worse. Now, don't think on it anymore. I'm off to get my beauty sleep," the meute stated matter-of-factly.

Green's belly rumbled. "Well, if everyone's comfy here, I'm going hunting—dragons need to eat a lot more than this," Green declared.

Before anyone could respond, he had thumped away.

The next morning, Sterling's shoulder ached from a night on the rocky cave floor, and his skin was peppered with purple sparkles. Leftover rabbit and onion stew simmered above a low-burning fire. Green snored underneath tiny emerald thunderclouds. Next to the fire, Barath slept soundly. His wooden facial features drooped pleasantly, and honeysuckle tea drippings pooled beneath his roots.

"Always a messy eater, that one," the wizard chuckled as he brewed a new potion with an extra hop in his step.

The cauldron's bubbling was a familiar sound by now, so Sterling didn't rush to watch the magic at first. Nevertheless, it was a surprise to see Thahn frolicking about his wizard's kitchen, meddling with potion ingredients so early. Sterling wanted to ask him where he had gone last night, how he'd gotten hurt (why was wizards' blood blue?), and how the healing crystals worked. But he knew wizards did as they pleased and only talked about their magic business when they wanted to. Besides, Thahn looked entirely healed—a dash too spritely for his age, even.

Ingredients sauntered into the cauldron, floating and bobbing at the potion wizard's command.

"A clump of winter pine tree moss and squirt of rocky mountain algae," he sang as the ingredients swirled and the mist churned above the sloshing magic concoction.

*That's where he went! He fetched the tree moss and the*

*mountain algae—probably ran into a mountain troll along the way.*

A handful of forest berries plunked to the bottom of the brew, followed by a snowy mountain falcon feather, then the fang of an ice-scale snake. Sterling shuddered at the thought of stark white scales slipping through innocent snow. He didn't know why, but he'd always hated snakes. He tried to ignore the slinky white streak slithering in the liquid—an unmistakable serpent shape.

The brew fizzed and spun faster, which meant, thankfully, it was nearly finished.

"And for the final touch, the elusive cloud mountain mist obtained by our magical dragon," the potion wizard said, with a proud smile toward Green.

Green gave a sleepy smile as he sat up and rubbed his eyes.

The wizard placed the ruby-red ring into an S-shaped glass tube. It rolled slowly, making its way through the tubing. As it dropped into the lower curve, the ring produced a small bubble. Floating above the cauldron, the bubble rose higher into the air. The potion wizard scampered to stand on a wobbly stool to reach it with his wand.

"Oof!" exclaimed the wizard, trying to keep his balance. "It's got a mind of its own!"

Sterling snatched up the makeshift bow he'd been crafting (there was not much to do inside the cave) and shot a wooden arrow straight toward the bubble.

It flew true, and the bubble popped, sprinkling its innards into the potion.

"Good work, young hunter—very precise shooting," the wizard said. The sound of approval in his voice reminded Sterling of his father.

Barath awoke in time to see the emergence of a gleaming stone with a snow-white cloud spinning inside. The cave went quiet.

The seven sisters spoke in unison: "Potion Wizard, you have created the Sky Stone. This was a difficult task, and you found the chosen one. You have done well to teach the dragon child his magic—he is the balance in your most important magic blend of all. But we must warn you that you are in danger—you are being hunted. The dark wizard searches the clouds and the sea for you. The other three stones must be made faster than planned. Seek an alliance with the creatures in your path—you will need their help if you are to succeed and if you all are to survive."

The potion wizard patted his mended robe, stained from his recent mysterious injury.

"Thank you, Sisters. I know just the creatures—I will do as you ask. Wizard's promise."

# CHAPTER TWENTY
# BLUE HUNTERS

It wasn't long before they reached the sandy shores of the Pearl Sea. Despite a swift and uncomplicated flight, their quest for rare aquamarine pearls was interrupted almost immediately. Sterling knew they'd be tracked, followed, and hunted. He assumed this was because of Green—that Jeanno wanted all dragons gone—but the truth was always more complicated. As soon as they landed, he'd searched the skies with his hunter vision and spotted Blue Herikats, a flock of sea-savvy centipars (their bodies were a mixture of predatory bird parts and big cats), in the distance. They didn't have much time to hide, so when the wizard had conjured a hollow sand dune, Sterling had shoved Green inside and set about disguising the hiding place. He hoped it was enough. Sterling and the wizard hurriedly buried themselves in sand, but Barath began muttering to himself, not budging from his place near a group of palm trees.

"I think they picked up the scent of us—our magic —near the Hills of Bryght and tracked us here," Sterling noted.

"Yes—the scent ends here at the shoreline where the land meets the sea," the wizard agreed. "You're right about that. You are a wise hunter."

The centipars descended upon the sandy shores like vultures swooping down to ravage a carcass. Two of the flying predators traversed the shallow seawater, their steel-colored eyes surveying every living creature while clawed feet dragged against the sand. The vibration stirred brittle fish and spiddlings (a tasty snack for the centipars), forcing them to spill out of their moist burrows. A third Blue Herikat darted away from the water toward a grove of palm trees, and a fourth disappeared into the sky beyond Sterling's hunter vision.

"One's coming this way, Barath!" Sterling warned, and counted his lucky stars that Green had been strong and fast enough to fly to the sea with Sterling on his back. It would have been nearly impossible to get Banefield to enter a sand dune; instead, he'd stayed at the cave, out of danger.

"Oh, brittle sticks and wizard bark!" Barath worried aloud. "Hurry, tree magic! Do your work!" His bark transformed, growing a coating of tropical tree fur, and his branches sprouted yellow-green palm leaves. Even a bundle of tiny coconuts grew beneath his canopy.

"He looks every bit a real palm tree, only smaller," muttered Green.

"Shhh!" The potion wizard motioned for silence.

Seconds later, a Blue Herikat prowled the palm tree grove.

*Sniff. Sniff.*

Barath's rapidly grown palm leaves rustled in the breeze, and he whispered a scent-cloaking enchantment. His disguise fooled the eyes, but the experienced centipar was adept at picking apart magic and nonmagic smells. Sterling held back a gag as Barath oozed a pungent, overly ripe coconut odor. Centipars were better hunters than Sterling realized. He scolded himself silently for not thinking to tell Barath to cover his scent sooner.

Rank coconut smell or not, the Blue Herikat walked toward Barath without hesitation. Clawed paws crushed tropical, yellow-spotted flowers and smashed sprigs of sand clover that sprouted in shady spots. A pair of eyes (more eagle than catlike) were laser-focused on the smallest (and smelliest) palm tree in the grove. Blue striped fur and pointed ears twitched as the Herikat inspected Barath.

*Please don't find me. Please don't chew me up and rip my branches to pieces.*

Sterling blinked, realizing he could hear the meute's thoughts because the magical tree was under intense duress. Meutes could disappear into their bark, making them look like any other tree, but this ability wouldn't last, and Barath was afraid.

*It's been too long since I've used my tree magic. I've relied on the potion wizard all these years for protection. The spell of similarity isn't fooling these savages,* Barath continued.

*Stop whining! You'll be fine. Just relax and sway in the salty breeze like all the other palm trees,* the potion wizard chimed into the magical inner-mind chatter. At Sterling's back, Green shifted uncomfortably. Sand had gotten in his nose, and he held his breath, trying not to sneeze.

*Scratch, scratch.*

Razor-sharp claws dug in the sand. A wet nose pressed against Barath's trunk.

*She's going to knock me over! I'm not a real palm tree—I can't take much more of this. I'm not even rooted!"* Barath screeched inside his mind.

His broad palm leaves swayed back and forth frantically. Green's sides heaved as he struggled against the sand.

A sneeze echoed from the sandy dunes, and Sterling seized his dagger. But it wasn't Green's sneeze. The Herikat shook her head and snorted once more. She turned silently and took to the skies.

"Thank Everen's stars." Barath sighed and wiped sap drippings from his forehead.

"They won't go far. They will hunt down the coastline and return here, where they started. Centipars always search the same place twice—they are thorough trackers," the potion wizard explained. "Now, the seabanes will be near the ocean floor where the aquamarine pearls grow. I will go and speak with them—alone."

Barath's palm tree form melted away until he looked like his stumpy, grumpy self again. His tree energy was depleted, and he faded into his bark.

"Old boy. He can't carry on without healing magic. I'll get to him when I return," the potion wizard said. "Sterling, stay here with him. Protect him if the centipars return while I'm away. Green, keep your tail ready to fly. Meet me in the deep water the second you see the seabanes surface but not a moment before."

Sterling and Green nodded in unison.

The potion wizard marched into the ocean. First, his cape changed to water form, then his cap and body. He was recognizable, though translucent and watery, before he splashed into the next wave. Then he was gone.

Sterling wasn't sure how he could protect Barath against a pack of Herikats with his dagger. And it wasn't as if he knew how to force his blood magic to leap out of his forearms and form red liquid weapons. There had to be a witch nearby to activate the battle instincts. Even then, he couldn't be sure what his blood would do, or who it would target if emerged without a witch to fight. He looked at Green. "Could you conjure up some of that handy green fire if I ask you to?"

"I think so," Green replied, wiggling his tail. It flashed crystal, then back to its usual emerald-green hue.

"What was it like to fight a witch?" Green sputtered.

Sterling's stomach hardened. He hadn't thought about his vile encounters with the dark sorceresses all day, but they regularly plagued his thoughts and dreams.

"Sorry, Sterling Fierce—I'm just nervous and, well, you must be awfully powerful to destroy something as magical as a witch. I was wondering if you could use your hunter magic against the Herikats?"

"It's okay. I just don't talk about that part of me—not out loud, really. Witches and witch hunters can sort of hear each other's thoughts, so I figured I'd not give them anything to hear," Sterling explained.

"Do you mean that there could be witches nearby—here, somewhere?" Green's voice began to tremble. His tail perked up and tilted, like it was listening to Sterling's every word.

"They could be anywhere, Green. It's hard to explain. When I fought them—even after they were destroyed or banished from our realm—I could still feel them. Something tells me witches never really die," he said aloud for the first time. His stormy gray eyes swirled, and his stomach cramped like he'd swallowed a bag of ice. His wrist pulsed. Then, his veins swelled, forming liquid ridges in a lightning pattern up his forearms.

*No, not now! Be calm,* he silently told his blood. He had no idea if his blood would listen, but he had to try.

Green's tail shook and dove into the Story Dragon's arms for comfort.

"Sorry, big guy. My hunter's blood can be activated if I think about them too much. This magic—it's ancient, like the battle between witches and witch hunters. I still have much to learn," Sterling admitted.

For what felt like an eternity, nothing but the sound of the sea filled the salty air as the pair sat in silence, waiting for the potion wizard's signal. Sterling monitored the shoreline the way his father had taught him to watch for predators. Green huddled next to the witch hunter, scanning the skies. Twice, Sterling caught a glimpse of a centipar in the distance, and each time, he began to sweat, wondering if he was really up to the task of protecting the young dragon at his side.

Finally, two seabanes, muscular with whale-like tails, splashed and broke the ocean's surface. Each carried a netted sack with a large sphere inside. Green activated his crystal tail and Sterling hopped on his back, cradling a faceless Barath. They flew toward the seabanes, but there was no sign of the potion wizard. Green swooped down to the ocean, so close that cold sprays of salt water spattered against their faces. He saw nothing beneath the endless blue waters.

"Tan-zahn!" The potion wizard gargled as he burst from the ocean depths.

*Poof.* The aquamarine pearls shrunk down to the size of two peas. They floated from the seabanes' nets and squeezed inside an enchanted locket around the potion wizard's neck.

"Thank you, my friends. And thank you for protecting the seas of Everen. Until we meet again," the potion wizard said to the seabanes.

The half-whale, half-human creatures thumped their thick chests with their flippers and grunted words in a language that Sterling and Green couldn't hope to understand.

They had accomplished their quest, but they had been found. All four Blue Herikats soared toward them like blue lightning bolts from the sky.

"Green, the fire!" Sterling called out, clutching his dagger. The young dragon concentrated on forming a flame in his hands, but as he did so, the crystals in his tail dimmed. Sterling held up his dagger, but the creature dodged neatly and raked its claws along Green's tiny wing. The young dragon yelped, and suddenly, they were falling toward the ocean.

A small explosion of green fire puffed overhead. Sterling's jaws clacked together as Green regained his balance and stopped midfall.

"They're coming around again." Sterling panted. "We've got to get out of here." He clutched Barath closer. Then the wizard was hovering next to him, dripping sea water onto Sterling's head.

There were four popping noises. Then the four centipars were falling from the sky, tangled in sea rope and coral netting. Catlike fangs gnawed free almost before the creatures could get wet. Deep snarls and growls bellowed in the wind as the creatures flocked to the skies once again.

"You're too late," the larger of the two seabanes grunted. "They are gone, and their scent is lost in the sea breeze. Leave and take your claws with you!" And it was true, the wizard was gone and had taken his companions without a trace.

Back in the cave without a name, Sterling helped bandage Green's wing, scowling at the potion wizard all the while. The injury wasn't deep. In fact, it was barely bleeding, but the young dragon whimpered and sobbed the whole time, his high-pitched voice echoing off the crystals in the cave.

Seemingly oblivious, the potion wizard poured his energy into a new brew. It simmered and moaned unlike any of the other potions. It sounded like it was in pain, whimpering at times, matching Green's sobs in intensity if not volume. When one aquamarine pearl slid into the cauldron, the moaning and whimpering hushed. The pearl bobbed up and down. As its shell melted layer by layer, the brew transformed into a beautiful teal paste. A singing came out of nowhere, and the mixture rolled over and over in the cauldron's center. Suddenly, a pearl-shell plate formed. Above it hovered a stone in the shape of a heart. Its edges bore a crisscross netting Sterling had seen in his Alin's books—it was the bandage stitching pattern used in very ancient healing spells.

Green was immediately distracted from his injuries.

"It's so fancy!" His eyes had grown bright again, a relief after their dull pallor of the previous hour.

The fifth stone snuggled into the cave's enchanted case next to its four siblings. Despite himself, Sterling couldn't help but admire it. The magic made his skin prickle when he stared at the stones for too long.

The seven sisters sang, "The Sea Stone has been reborn! Our strength is returning. Find what you need in the Cannabie Desert. The dunes hold sandstone secrets, but beware. The battle of the sands is blinding. Look to the clouds if you become lost."

"Yes, thank you, Sisters. Now, I must attend to my loyal companion." The potion wizard scuttled over to Barath. The tiny tree lay in a tub of a healing brew, which had not helped a bit.

"He's not come back to life, not even close," Green worried aloud.

"Ah, the sea is powerful. The pearls—the purest of the sea," the potion wizard said as he placed the second aquamarine pearl into the healing bath.

The milky white potion seeped into Barath's bark.

"Can I have some?" Green stretched out his wing.

"That's not the damaged one, little guy," Sterling informed him. Green turned, and sure enough, the scratched wing was still tucked against his body.

"Healing is a slow business," the potion wizard spoke softly, patting the top of Barath's trunk. "We'll know by morning if the sea pearl was the right choice."

Barath looked as unresponsive as a dried-up starfish washed up to shore, and Sterling didn't feel any life-force from his brittle trunk body.

Green crouched beside the tiny meute. "I miss him —even if he's grouchy."

Sterling sat beside Green and softly scratched his dragon scales, remembering that Green was just a child (a large, magical, sharp-toothed one). Still, this must have been hard for him. He had no other dragons—no parents. Sterling knew what it felt like not to belong—to be alone and without his parents. He closed his eyes and didn't bother wiping the sandy tears that ran down his chin.

# CHAPTER TWENTY-ONE

# MIDNIGHT DINNER

The potion wizard's cave was full of seasoned cauldron smells and crystal dust. It was dark and damp—so different from Green's dragon home with sky windows and sunlight. He tossed and turned that night. Being an Air Dragon, he craved fresh wind and a view of the sky. So he decided to sneak out of the cave, tiptoeing as delicately as a dragon could. He followed the path of the moonlight, careful not to wake Sterling, Barath, or the wizard. He'd noticed the witch hunter twitching on the cave floor, having some sort of dream. When he'd first met Sterling, Green had been afraid of the witch hunter. After all, ever since the Battle of Flames when the Fire Dragons had attacked Everen, humans and dragons had been enemies. But seeing Sterling now, Green couldn't help but feel they had been destined to become friends.

Green left the cave behind and took a satisfying

breath of forest air. It smelled of tree bark and wet mud—it was glorious! He ventured into the nearby forest, which was bursting with an assortment of trees. Despite the nightfall, deep pockets of greenish-blue and black-barked trees were visible.

"It's beautiful," Green thought aloud, inspecting the quiet, shadowed landscape.

A narrow stream divided the land, and soft grassy patches popped out of the shallow water as they pleased. The current flowed with remarkable speed for its size, tumbling over riverbed stones and jagged strands of soil. The scent of fresh plants and mud settled his nerves. He rested, lying on his round belly, and studied glowpillars inching up and down the exposed muddy banks at the stream's edge. Invisible legs moved in a front-to-back pattern, moving their tiny bodies forward inch by inch. They had grown fat from nibbling on small white eggs buried in the wet dirt. One overly plump fellow leaned too far and plopped down into the water.

Green imagined a protection bubble in his mind like he'd seen the potion wizard conjure, and he sprinkled water droplets from the stream onto his scales. He closed his eyes and concentrated until a tiny bubble formed around the glowpillar. It busied its legs trying to climb the side of the bubble, not real-izing it had been saved from drowning.

"I've got you, little one," Green said, grinning. His Story Dragon magic worked like a charm!

Green blew a short dragon's breath, releasing the tiny creature over the lush grass with a pop.

"Even small acts of kindness can change our future," a familiar voice said.

Green's belly heaved, and he spun around.

"Bah! Where did you come from, hunter?" He was genuinely surprised that Sterling had managed to sneak up on him—dragons had impeccable hearing.

"I know my way around the woods. And besides, you woke me up when you stomped out of the cave. You aren't exactly soft on your feet," Sterling said with a smirk.

"Hush puppies and pork pie. You were fast asleep, drooling on the cave floor! I didn't wake you. You must've had a bad dream," Green said.

"Hunters never sleep deep; we're always aware of our surroundings." Sterling shook his head, trying to rid himself of the whispers of a hunter's vision that had plagued him without really giving him more information. "So, what's your plan? Make a cooking fire, fall asleep under the stars? That cave gets to me too—it's dark, breathless. But I can relax out here," Sterling admitted, stretching his arms over his head.

Green sighed. "Didn't have a plan, but that sounds as good as any."

Sterling collected loose scrapple weeds, and Green gathered fallen branches. Together, they built a good-sized cooking fire. It crackled and glowed with natural, nonmagical light. Soon, roasted mudfish and

STERLING FIERCE AND THE LOST DRAGONS   139

spotted mushrooms dripped and sputtered over the flames, giving off a pleasing aroma.

"Dragons love meats of all kinds, but fish is my favorite. I'll eat fish as often as I can get my paws on it," Green said through a mouthful.

"Lucky for you, I can catch as many fish as you want. Always had a knack for fishing. We'll have full bellies tonight!" Sterling said.

They chewed contentedly for a moment.

"Hey, Green, I was wondering something. If there was another way, something we could do to help your parents—all the dragons. But it would be risky, and it might not work. Do you think you'd want to try it?"

The dragon's tail perked up and bent toward Sterling.

"Well, I'd do anything to save them," Green admitted. "But the potion wizard already has a plan, and he's wise and experienced in this sort of thing—there are even books about him."

"I don't think Thahn is wrong..." Sterling paused. "But I don't really know what his plan is. No one has even tried to talk to Jeanno. What if there's a better way? Maybe we could offer him a trade—something else in exchange for returning the dragons. Usually when people do drastic things, it's because they need something. Maybe we could help him get what he needs, and he'll turn back from the dark," Sterling said.

Green's eyes were wide with excitement.

"I miss my mom and dad so much. Do you think

this plan would work? What in Everen do we have that he'd want?"

Sterling felt a wave of sweat forming across his forehead as he went into his best selling-pecans-at-the-village-market type of pitch.

"The stones," he replied as his throat went dry.

Green's tail darted behind the dragon. "No. No, we can't do that to the potion wizard—not after all he's done for us. And Jeanno may not even want the stones."

"Oh, he'd want them—and we'd just have to give him two. Think about it. The Mountain Stone is known by the ancients as 'Mountain's Breath.' He wants power, right? To rule over his own kingdom? Well, he could use this stone to create his own land—anywhere in the ocean as far as away from Everen as he can get (preferably). Boom! An instant island just for him. Now, add in the Forest Stone. This one gives life. So, he could create his own race of followers to worship him and follow his every command. He gets supreme power over his own realm, and he leaves Everen. And the dragons get to come home. Even Jeanno couldn't resist," Sterling said, looking more confident than he felt.

"I don't know, Sterling. It could work, but I don't think Thahn will give up the stones," Green finally admitted.

"Green, buddy, if Jeanno declines our trade, then we hightail it back here—nobody would know. Besides, Thahn is using an old solution, and it might be time to use a new, fresher idea," Sterling said, believing in his idea more than ever.

Green sniffled. "You really think we can get my mom and dad back?"

"I'll do whatever it takes," Sterling said, and he meant it more than anything else he'd said so far.

## CHAPTER TWENTY-TWO
## A TWISTED LAIR

With both the wizard and Barath asleep, it was the task of a minute for Sterling to slip into the cave and take the Mountain and Forest Stones. They rested heavily in his pocket as Green flew them north toward the Isle of Marble and Maze. In the dark, Sterling peered over what was otherwise a deserted isle and was grateful they could fly up to the wizard's lair instead of climbing through the crumbly rocks below.

Jeanno's lair was easy to spot; a squat tower rose from the tallest point on the island, its base cluttered with smaller buildings and entrances to caves. Sterling peered into the gloomy rock walls and tried to pick one where Green would be safe to land. They settled on a large opening a fair distance from the tower and far from any scents of centipar.

"I'll go scout ahead." Sterling felt the need to whisper, even though he was sure no one else was in earshot.

"But what if something comes?" Green whimpered.

"You'll have to stay hidden. I'll keep watching, and if I see any green flame, I'll hurry back. But as long as you're quiet, no one should notice you."

Green agreed reluctantly, and Sterling began climbing up the nearby rocks. He was pleased to find a staircase shortly after, and although he took care to avoid being seen, everything was silent. It was as if no one lived on the island at all.

Finally, he spotted a brightly lit window overhead. He clambered up a convenient scraggly tree and peered inside. The room was immediately recognizable as the laboratory from his hunter's vision. It was round and cluttered with strange implements and magical ingredients, but it appeared to be empty of life.

The door clanged as a wizard walked in, black curly hair bobbing.

"My newest creation is nearly complete. It feels almost as satisfying as watching those giant reptiles disappear from the map. We're setting the magic realm back to its rightful state. I tell you, Smauteken, it's time for the great wizards to come forth and enjoy their might as they once did." The wizard tinkered with his complicated machinery, speaking aloud as if he had an audience.

*Jeanno the Twisted.*

Sterling stared at the wizard they'd been trying so hard to thwart. Grease smudges covered Jeanno's clammy hands, and his robe sleeves were littered with burn marks. For some time, it was quiet as he worked on his machinery—just the sounds of clicks and chirps and clanks until a gigantic "Ah-choo" bellowed from the corner of the room.

Jeanno shot a grimace toward a wolf-sized worm with floor-length hair and shiny white eyes.

"Must you make those incessant body noises while I am crafting!?"

"Sorry, boss. It's all the electricity. It frizzes my worm hairs when you work on that metal ball thingy," said Smauteken.

"I'm sure you'll learn to manage them quietly, you hairy oaf. There's always a price to pay for success. Remember, I've already paid my dues." The dark wizard patted his face.

Jeanno's eye socket held a floating mechanical sphere where his left eye should have been. Its silver exterior held a black-and-red pupil in the middle, surrounded by a protective coating of enchanted glass.

"A small sacrifice for the seeing spell, and its vision is more advanced than the original. Night sight, magic detection. Even the laser turned out satisfactory."

Smauteken rubbed one of his burned worm feet (they looked more like rug tassels) against another and grimaced.

"Jeanno! Jeanno!" Sterling clutched the branch

tighter as three voices chimed in. "Our friends have spotted the potion wizard and a meute companion traveling together. It was them this time—we're sure of it," three ink flies tattled in unison as they wisped into the small stone laboratory, bumbling into one another.

Wings flickered with sparks of light, and three sets of bubbled eyes followed the dark wizard's every move. Their plump bodies glowed in shades of purple that Sterling didn't recognize. Had he been closer, he'd have reached out to touch them—their pig-sized bodies were alluring, begging to be admired.

"My darling insect spies, it's so good to finally see you. But I must know, how can you be sure it's my nemesis and his overgrown talking root and not some other common wizard-meute pair?" Jeanno plucked a wrench from his workbench. "Did your friends have the wit to inspect closely? No wild-goose chases this time, I presume?"

The brightest-colored ink fly cleared her throat. "Er, um. Yes, Your Greatness. They can be trusted. We're sure it's the pair you seek. They went deep into the Bear Woods. Our cousins followed until they magicked beneath the ground. They were hunting for something."

"That sounds suspiciously delightful. What else?" Jeanno asked, arching a midnight-black eyebrow.

The middle-sized ink fly spoke. "He was nervous, very nervous. He checked the forest—his wizard's cap nearly fell off from swiveling about—checking behind his tracks. He must've gotten what he came for. He hightailed it out of there—only left a puff of smoke behind."

"Now, girls, you've failed me before. How many more of your family and friends must you lose to the lighting box before your accuracy improves? I'm curious." Jeanno turned his back to his flying guests, seeming unimpressed. He rummaged through bins until he found the precise dropper he wanted. He applied metallic drippings at various angles to the shiny device in his hand while ink flies fluttered their wings nervously.

"You're not released from your servitude until the potion wizard is found. And I'd like to teach that ill-mannered walking tree root a lesson he'll never forget —Barath something or other. Once I have them both, you three will be free of your debt to me. Wizard's promise." Jeanno smirked.

*This guy...doesn't seem all that reasonable.*

Sterling spotted the youngest ink fly sweeping piles of purple droppings beneath a storage cabinet. Ink flies tended to shed (or rather, leak) when they were afraid or in danger.

Smauteken sat upright, his front worm feet dangling in the air. "What happens next, boss? Snack time comin' up soon?" The pudgy worm nibbled on cornbread crumbs that had gotten stuck in the hair around his mouth.

The ink flies twitched back and forth, awaiting

Jeanno's next command. But he was enamored with his new mechanical creation.

"What happens next is the beauty of engineering and my dedication to its precise science. This seeking machine will tell me where any magic abnormalities lie anywhere in Everen. From the seas to the skies and mountaintops, I'll see it all," he cackled.

He turned the crank and entered a series of codes into the main screen. The seeking machine floated a foot or two into the air. It clicked, then sputtered, finally humming as its inner workings clinked into place, spinning. This was followed by flashing lights and hissing before it clunked and thumped to a furious stop. A map of black lines and shapes sketched the topography of Everen. Slowly, glowing dots lit up the Isle of Marble and Maze, as well as every wizard city one by one.

"It's working! Smauteken, look at this sheer genius right in front of you! Stop thinking only of your next meal, you useless oaf. This is the future. Oh—what's this? Curious. Do you see the orange lights?"

"Mmm. They look more peach than orange, boss—like tiny peaches. Yum," Smauteken said, smacking his lips.

Jeanno slammed his fist on the workbench table. "Imbecile! Don't you see?! With this seeking machine, the most magical and powerful ingredients are here—I have their location at my talented fingertips. The potion wizard fool is after the spell to awaken the seven sisters. They'll turn up at these locations—here on the map. Girls, fetch the centipars and send them to the White Mountains, the Eastlands—the volcanoes. Hurry! Grobbenses' Tower—tell the Blue Herikats stationed there to double their patrols. Tell them all to track the potion wizard and his meute; the first to find them will be rewarded beyond measure."

The hairy worm had inched his way beneath a wooden workbench, eyes squeezed shut.

"We will not fail you, Your Greatness," the three ink flies buzzed at once in perfect harmony. They darted out of the stoic laboratory, away from the stench of metal and machine oil. Their purple lights blinked rapidly, and hexagon wings fluttered as fast as they could.

## CHAPTER TWENTY-THREE
# A SPLINTERED IDEA

Sterling had seen enough. If Jeanno's goal was to stop the potion wizard, Sterling could offer him something he wanted. He wasn't sure how to begin negotiations but going through a door seemed like a good place to start. He glanced over his shoulder, but there was no sign of a frightened Story Dragon, so he took the chance and ducked through the nearest doorway.

Like the laboratory, the entrance was cluttered and unkempt. Old boots and delivery crates littered the area except for a narrow path weaving among the debris. Sterling tread carefully, but he could still hear Jeanno shouting overhead:

"Genius. My work is genius, striking on the verge of insanity—yet, it's so underappreciated—for now."

Sterling crept to an inner door and pushed it open a crack. It led to a filthy kitchen littered with unwashed dishes and greasy kitchen gadgets. The next room had once been a dining room, and further along, there was a dusty library. Sterling finally found the stairs. Jeanno's voice grew louder again, echoing from a room at the end of the upstairs hall.

Sterling ducked into an alcove and took a deep breath. He'd been so sure this was the right plan, but something didn't feel right. He took the two stones from his pocket and let them rest in his palms. They glowed faintly, radiating a gentle warmth. Sterling ran his finger over his upper lip. The little mustache reminded him of his father. What would Sir Rider Fierce have done?

"Why would you bring those here?" a voice rasped.

Sterling jumped, nearly dropping the stones. He peered into the shadows above his head and caught the faintest gleam of an iron birdcage. Two spindly hands were clutching at the bars, and a set of frail leaves poked out around the top.

"A meute?"

"No time for that, human. You must take those stones away from here."

"You don't understand. I'm here to save the dragons."

"I guessed you were stupid for coming here to begin with, but only a complete idiot would think bringing those stones here is anything short of lunacy."

Sterling rolled his eyes. Meutes were all rude. He began to slide toward the laboratory door.

"Wait, please?" The small tree's plaintive whisper drew Sterling up short. From his new vantage point, he could see that the cage's bars cut cruelly into the meute's bark. Why would Jeanno keep his companion locked up like this?

"Are you hurt?" he whispered. His hand went to his knife. "I can get you out of there."

"No point. Jeanno will just lock me up again. He hates wisdom from any source, even if it's one that helps guide his magic."

"Then we'll get you away from here. Come with me."

The meute tried to shake its head, but the bars of the cage were too tight. A few splinters dropped from the cage, catching in Sterling's hair. "Don't you know anything? I can't leave my wizard. We're bonded now. If I leave him, I'll die."

Sterling's eyes grew wide. "I can't just abandon you here." Now that he was looking, he could clearly see dozens of burns and scratches. The meute's nose had been gouged away, and his legs were twisted under him in an excruciating pose.

"Water," the meute replied. He shut his eyes and pointed. A pitcher and cup had been set on a high shelf just out of reach of his trembling grasp. Sterling leaped to fill the cup and pass it to the meute, who slowly trickled drops over his rootlike feet. The young hunter whirled to face the laboratory once more, this time with rage.

Before he could react, a high-pitched voice buzzed from the room. It was an ink fly.

"The centipars are on their way! You were right about the Story Dragon—he is with them! And a human boy," one announced.

"The packs are already out tracking them—they are the best hunters in all the land. You will have your prize."

"We are tired and wish to be set free now. Please release us from your servitude," one begged.

Sterling shoved the stones into his pockets. The wizard had a magic tracker. No doubt the surplus of magic on the island was the only thing disguising Green's. Sterling tried to control his breathing. He'd led his little brother into a trap.

Jeanno's voice echoed again.

"More plotting magic doers? I'll need them all out of the way. No, no, girls—you are in debt to me until I have this disruptive foursome in my grasp. But you've all come back empty-handed."

There was a boom, and smoke curled from the crack under the laboratory door. Then there was a small cry of despair and the sounds of chains rattling.

"It's a trade, my dear—the potion wizard's crew for your sisters' lives. I'm being more than fair this time," Jeanno said.

Muffled screams echoed against the stone walls.

"They are the only family I have left. You really are twisted," the fly sputtered. There was a buzz, then silence.

"Say, boss, you aren't gonna hurt the fly girls, are ya?" Smauteken asked.

"That depends on the youngest sibling—she knows what to do. She just needs the right...motivation," Jeanno cackled. "With those insects and the centipars hunting my nemesis and this beautiful piece of metal genius to find the Story Dragon, I cannot lose. I'll find them all and destroy them, one by one if I must."

"I'm not feeling hungry anymore. I'm going to do a bit of thinking," said the hairy worm.

The door creaked open, and Sterling flattened himself against the side of the alcove, but Smauteken didn't even look up as he shuffled past. Sterling took a long look at the worm's frazzled hair and realized that Jeanno had been experimenting on the poor creature. There would be no trading with the dark wizard. But if the tracking device could truly find Green, Sterling had to do something to stop it.

He crept toward the door, which Smauteken had left ajar. Inside the lab, Jeanno was poring through a thick book on a side table. The magic tracker was humming in the center of the room. Sterling peered at it, scratching his head. One of the wood chips that had fallen from the meute scraped his finger. He flinched, but then he had an idea.

The gears were delicate. A splinter in just the right spot might be enough to break it. Sterling took a deep breath, focused all his skill as a hunter, and threw the tiny chunk of wood. The gadget's lights turned from juicy peach to fire red, and the whole contraption began to shake. Jeanno's head whipped around, but Sterling was already down the hall and scurrying for the back exit. He hoped he'd bought them enough time.

After a few minutes, Sterling slowed, he'd lost track of which staircase he needed to follow and had ended up at the beach. There was a noise, and Sterling ducked behind an outcrop, trying to catch his breath.

Then he saw the small ink fly sitting alone on the shore next to the ocean. She wept. And she wept more until her purple tears puddled in the sand.

"Hey, what's all this purple goo?" came a voice from the sand.

"W-who's under there?" the fly asked, edging away from the purple puddle.

"It is Smauteken, of course, and you're leaking into my burrow," he said.

A round, hairy head popped out of the sand. It was covered in plum-colored drippings.

The ink fly giggled.

"It's only you. I'm troubled, Smauteken. Wizard business isn't my business, but I must find the potion wizard. I don't know how, and even if I found him, I couldn't make him and his friends go to Jeanno. Jeanno will harm them. I know he will—you don't know the awful things he's done, or you wouldn't stay. You have a choice. But if I don't do as he commands, I'll never see my sisters alive again," she said, sniffling.

"I've been thinking about things, as worms do. We aren't known for bravery, but if it's all the same for you, I could come along. I've no wings to fly, but if you could manage to carry me...? Besides, I can do the talking when we find this other wizard. I like wizards," Smauteken said as he licked his hair, sticking it to the side of his round face like a plump green grape wrapped in fur. Sterling tensed. The worm didn't seem dangerous, but the idea of these creatures trailing them gave him goosebumps.

"Thank you, Smauteken. That would be lovely, and I promise not to cry on you anymore if you promise not to like wizards so much," the ink fly said.

The two began putting together a sling so that the fly could carry Smauteken easily, and Sterling crept back up the trail. He concentrated, trying to remember where he had come in, but it was long past midnight, and everything was dark. He wandered along the paths, trying to focus his hunter's sight.

"Come on, just show me a hint of Green," he muttered. Then he saw a bright flash of green flame. His heart fell as he realized it wasn't his hunter's sight but a dragon distress call. He broke into a sprint, taking the stairs three at a time.

He reached the cave mouth just as Green came barreling out.

"Sterling!" the dragon gasped, catching his friend in his arms. Then they were airborne.

"What happened? What did you see?"

"I don't know! It had so many legs, though!"

Sterling looked back. The island was already out of sight, but he was sure it wouldn't be the last they'd see of Jeanno or his minions.

# CHAPTER TWENTY-FOUR

# EXPECTED GUESTS

W hen they arrived back at the cave, the wizard was already packing.

"Wizard, sir," Green started, his squeaky voice echoing among the crystals in the ceiling, "we went to this island, and now there's a bug and some monsters chasing us, and we've got to get away."

"Quite right. Please go pack up the books I've left on the table." The wizard gestured to a section of the cave just out of sight of his kitchen. He continued putting herbs into pouches and wrapping bottles. The box that had held the stones was completely empty. Sterling swallowed.

"Potion Wizard, sir?" he stuttered. Thahn paused, took a deep breath, then turned to face him.

Sterling couldn't meet his bright eyes behind the half-moon spectacles. Instead, he fished in his pockets and pulled out the stones. "You were right. Jeanno...I wanted to give him a chance, but this wouldn't have worked. I'm sorry I took the stones, and I'm sorry I doubted you."

The wizard's warm hands closed over Sterling's. He blinked up at Thahn's pained expression.

"I know, young Fierce. I knew it wouldn't work. Yet I hoped I was wrong." He stared into Sterling's eyes for another long minute. "But all is not lost. Come, I believe you have a horse to saddle, and if I'm not mistaken, we have some guests."

Sterling's heart clenched, but the wizard just grinned.

Banefield was contentedly munching some oat mash the wizard had conjured for him when Green met Sterling outside.

"I'm so tired," the young dragon moaned.

"I'm sorry, Green, I shouldn't have kept you out all night."

"Well, I slept some while I was waiting for you." His eyes widened at the stricken look on Sterling's face. "But I wasn't in danger. I woke up right away when that thing came."

"I'm glad you're alright. I shouldn't have left you."

Green whirled around. "Did you hear that?"

Sterling strained his ears. Something was bumbling in the shrubs nearby. Banefield glanced up from his breakfast.

"It's probably nothing," Sterling said.

A twig snapped from the weight of something or someone heavy.

Green looked at Sterling with wide eyes. "I'll conjure a ball of green flames just in case."

Suddenly, there was a fluttering noise, and two pale white eyes glowed inside a bush nearby.

"Ee-yah!" Green sent his fireball spinning toward the commotion.

"No, Green!" Sterling shouted.

But it was too late. Emerald flames burst into leafy curtains, setting the shrubs ablaze. There were shrieks and then voices rumbling from behind the burning bushes.

Sterling's senses heightened, catching the strange voices he wouldn't have been able to hear otherwise.

"I told you dragons are mean-spirited, foul beasts! He won't help us. Hurry, let's go before he eats us or burns us to ashes. We shouldn't have come," said a deep, shaky voice.

A high-pitched voice responded, "You're wrong. He will help us; my sisters said so. Besides, we have no choice. Jeanno will see to it that we are destroyed if we don't."

Sterling recognized their voices from the beach. "We won't hurt either of you if you promise to do the same. Can you put out the fire, Green?"

Green blew a gust of wind breath, and the fire fizzled out.

Darting from behind the charred bush, a pig-sized creature fluttered her wings in the emerald smoke.

"Since when is dragon fire any kind of a greeting?" The youngest ink fly bobbed up and down, glaring at the Story Dragon through her pulsing crystal-like eyes.

Green kinked his head to the side. "I don't know what kind of creature this one is, but she's mean," he said.

"She's brave. I'll give her that. Now, the other creature—where's your friend?" Sterling asked.

A hairy glob peeked from around the corner but refused to come farther.

"You've had a long journey. How about a snack?" Sterling offered some corn and oatmeal from Banefield's stash.

"I've never seen a dragon before. I thought you'd perch from above and peck at me with your beak," the worm said. He slumped closer and slowly put a corncob into his mouth. He was a rare sort of worm, bulky with round sections all connected into one globby body—not to mention the largest worm species that Sterling had ever seen. He had ten or twelve tiny feet that operated on their own, some sleeping on the ground while others moved about or dangled in the air.

"Oh, I don't have a beak, and I've never wanted to try worm. My cousins, the Fire Dragons or the Sand Dragons, they might," Green admitted.

"He's a Story Dragon," said Sterling. "The last of the dragons, at the moment."

"But the potion wizard is going to try to bring the dragons back. He's a good wizard," Green explained.

"Good or bad, magic is dangerous," the ink fly

spoke up. "I am trying to rescue my sisters. Jeanno the Twisted captured them."

"He took my family too. Maybe we can work together. I'm Green."

"I can see that," the fly observed.

"That's also his name," Sterling explained.

"And who are you, human?" the ink fly inquired. Her wings flashed electric purple. Sterling resisted the urge to reach out and touch her mesmerizing flickering.

"I'm just a hunter trying to stay on the good side of a bad situation."

"That's Sterling Fierce. He's a witch hunter—he's got magic blood," Green said with a gloating smile.

"Smauteken here," the hairy worm mumbled around the food in his mouth. "I've never left my island before. Jeanno took care of me after a dragon made a big flood that took my family. Dragons attacked him too—one tried to freeze him when he was a boy. But he wasn't kind to the ink flies. So I decided to help Saja. She's tiny but fearless."

"He's a worm full of thoughts—and food. I am Saja. I may be a small ink fly, but I'm a fast flyer and can carry ten times my body weight," Saja said. "And I will save my sisters, no matter what I must do—with or without your help."

"Well, then it's settled," said Sterling. "You'll both come with us back to the cave. We have a lot to talk about, and besides, there are more introductions in order."

Sterling led the way into the cave without a name. His lungs chilled as he once again breathed in the damp air. An echo of glass clinking rang from the kitchen, and he headed toward it. Saja and Smauteken entered the cave, hiding in Sterling's shadow. Green positioned himself behind the odd pair. Saja's wings buzzed, and Smauteken chewed his lower lip as they descended into the darkness, illuminated only by the purple glow of the crystals hanging from above.

"Ah, I've been expecting you; though, I must say I thought our meeting would be in the sands," the potion wizard said, tidying up his brewing tools. "Now, everything is neat enough. No sense in fussing over it anymore." He appeared pleased with his efforts and wiped at a sparkling bead of sweat below the rim of his cap. Then, with a swish of his wand, glittering sprinkles whispered over the wizard's kitchen, coating every bit with crystal dust.

The room disappeared.

"Whoa! Nice magic trick," Smauteken said, widening his pale eyes.

Saja fluttered past the hairy worm, scrutinizing the space where the potion wizard's kitchen had been just seconds before.

"It's all nearly invisible. So long as none of it sprouts legs and moves about, my beautiful brewing cookware will be safe from prying eyes," the potion wizard said.

"His magic seems more useful—better-spirited than the boss," Smauteken whispered to Saja.

"We'll see. Remember, wizards are powerful. Too powerful for their own good," Saja replied.

"Potion Wizard, I'd like you to meet Smauteken and Saja," Sterling started, unsure what else to say to introduce them properly. A flicker of shame resurfaced at the thought that the wizard would have to leave his kitchen behind now that Jeanno was on their trail.

The potion wizard winked at Sterling and then turned his attention to his two new guests.

"I really must know how a nightshade worm and an ink fly found my Story Dragon. This island is not on any map—I expect his magic drew you here?" He scanned Saja and Smauteken, his silver eyebrows raised high enough to lift his wizard's cap. His hat glowed briefly, and for a moment, Sterling felt a tingle in his belly, the kind he didn't like.

"I—um," Smauteken scratched the hairs on his head and looked at Saja. "My head feels funny."

"He's reading our thoughts!" Saja burst out crying. Drops of purple puddled beneath her. "I just hate wizards and all their tricks!"

The potion wizard conjured a wing warmer for the ink fly. It hovered toward her, landing perfectly on her delicate wings.

"Ah yes, well, we haven't time to get to know each other properly, I'm afraid. I am sorry for what Jeanno did to you and your sisters, Saja. Smauteken, I am sorry for the way he's mistreated you. He's not a kind or good wizard. Now, I plan to return every dragon and set things right in the magic world. Then I will see to it that your sisters are set free. But I will need you and Smauteken to stay with us the rest of our journey."

Before the pair could respond, a grumbling came from the oval nook in the cave wall, followed by clattering and banging. Then, a muttering tree stump covered in palm leaves emerged.

"Barath! You're okay!" Green exclaimed.

"I can't see two inches in front of me. These pesky palm leaves—and I had to sleep on coconuts covered in itchy hair! All the things I put up with," Barath complained as he waddled toward the group, scratching his side bark.

He didn't get far before Green smothered him in hugs.

Sterling patted Barath's back and brushed the palm leaves from his eyes. "I'm glad you're okay."

"I'll live. But this tropical look is a disaster," Barath squawked.

The potion wizard gave a knowing glance to Sterling before waving his wand. Barath's leaves were whirled and chopped into shorter, more manageable chunks.

"There, there. Much better, ol' boy. I think it's a fine look!" the potion wizard said with a playful grin.

Barath blinked his wooden eyelids. "Well, is

anyone going to tell me why there's a furry worm and a flying plum in our cave?"

Saja narrowed her eyes at Barath.

"Yes, yes. All part of the plan. Saja and Smauteken came to help. They will accompany us on our journey to find the rarest yet of the seven stone ingredients—the Sandstone of Time—and they'll want to see the dragons' return," the potion wizard said.

"Very well. At least there will be more of us—they can't shoot us all down," Barath declared.

Smauteken gulped. "Shoot us...down? What in the worm's world have I gotten into?"

Saja fluttered near Smauteken and patted one of his tiny, furry legs.

"We band together—all of us," said Sterling. "It's the only way. Besides, we'll pack plenty of snacks for the ride." He winked at Smauteken.

## CHAPTER TWENTY-FIVE
# THE LOST CITY OF TERRA

Flying over the Elvish territory, the expansive Bryght Hills, was relaxing. Green soared through the air behind the potion wizard and Saja. She was carrying Smauteken in a bundle of crystal dust mixed with her own webbing—ink flies were closely related to silk spiders, it turned out, only much larger. Barath nestled into the potion wizard's knapsack, and Sterling rode Banefield, who'd become accustomed to flying by now.

"It's a shame this flight enchantment is temporary, boy. You're a natural!" Sterling praised. He always felt like he was home when he rode his horse, even if Banefield was not really his but had been lent to him by Tomorak back home.

They dipped into valleys full of rich soil, wide rivers, and packs of wild ponies on the roam. Farmers below tended to colorful gardens, and straw-thatched rooftops snuggled into the hillsides. Tiny cooking fires sent smoke twirling upward with savory hints of roasted goat. The occasional beam of sunlight warmed Sterling's back as the sun rose.

Finding the Cannabie Desert was easy. It was an eyesore—a colorless patch at the intersection of the majestic purple mountains of the Vionin Kingdom, the wet green of the swamplands, and the lava fields of the Eastern Rocklands. Green farmland and colorful villages faded behind the travelers. The ground cracked and spilled outward, dry like water-less beaches. Rolling sand dunes rippled. An odd cluster of sand holes and remnants of campsites appeared out of nowhere and then vanished. Sterling scanned the area, but it was just endless sand humps littering a flat desert floor.

"We'll stop to eat soon? I'm terribly hungry. Can we take a tiny meal stop?" Smauteken begged.

The potion wizard whispered something to Bane-field. Sterling was whisked off his steed and into a flight bubble as his horse turned and flew away.

"This means we're going somewhere dangerous—too dangerous for horses," Sterling whispered. "And we're close because these flight bubbles don't last long!"

"Here comes the next part of our adventure, my young hunter," the potion wizard chuckled. He swooped down toward valleys lined with deep auburn sandstone, then plunged lower again. Green followed, then Saja (still hauling Smauteken), and Sterling's bubble sauntered behind. Soon, Saja's wings fluttered so ferociously that they surrounded her like a bubble. She darted out in front, keeping a close pace with the potion wizard. Suddenly, she disappeared, blending into the sand.

"She sure can hide when she wants. How clever!" the potion wizard remarked.

Everyone else landed, some more gracefully than others.

"My feetsies! This sand burns—I won't have any foot hairs left! Saja, come back!" Smauteken whined, trying to climb up Green's back with all twenty-four wriggling legs. "This isn't like my island—no seawater or moist sand to burrow beneath."

"Easy, fella!" Green wiggled his crystal tail and hovered back into the air.

Saja appeared without her magical bubble and perched on Sterling's shoulder. She was lighter than he might have guessed by looking at her. "Are there no plants or desert flowers with nectar to drink? My wings will dry out if we stay too long," she explained.

"Everyone remain calm. Now, for the tricky bit," said the potion wizard with a keen eye, searching for something.

Smauteken gasped. "I thought that *was* the tricky part!"

Sterling noticed the potion wizard was more cautious than he had been on any other ingredient-hunting quest.

Then he couldn't see anything but sand. A sandstorm had appeared as if from nowhere.

"I can't see!" Green wailed.

Sterling coughed through billowing red smoke. "What's happening?"

The dunes looked to be on fire, and black cannon-balls whizzed through the air. Sand bombs exploded all around them, digging craters into the brick-orange sand.

It was then that Sterling caught sight of them—hooded figures with glassy eyes moving in packs. They hurled cannonballs over their heads.

*Who are they?* Sterling's racing heart pummeled his ribcage.

"A sand army—not sure which faction," Barath mumbled, shaking his head. "Shouldn't have come..."

Scurrying for safety, Green activated his crystal tail.

"No," the potion wizard shouted over the commotion. "The air is too dangerous now. Focus, Story Dragon. Use your magic."

Green tried to concentrate, but just then, the buzzing of creatures on the other side of the valley rang out. A flurry of pointed legs stabbed the sand, flinging more debris into the hazy sky.

"Sand spiders!" Sterling warned.

"They're not here for us. The two sides are battling one another—this is war. Best to stay out of it," the potion wizard said, stuffing Barath into his robe's oversized pocket. "Focus, Story Dragon. We haven't much time," the potion wizard repeated in a tone much too calm for the situation.

"I still can't see," Green whimpered.

Just then, Saja swooped near the Story Dragon and fluttered her wings so fast that a patch of air cleared before his eyes. He flicked his tail, tossing sand over his scales, and he imagined a river of sand digging into the valley rock.

The sandy floor opened, exposing an underground door.

"Excellent magic-finding skills, Green, my boy! You've found the entrance to the hidden city of Terra —far from this mess. Off we go!" the potion wizard shouted.

One by one, they descended into the secret stone tunnels, leaving the thunderous war above. The path was made of stone on all sides, and it was pitch-black aside from the glowing crystal on the wizard's staff. The air grew cold and still as the tunnels wound even deeper.

"What if we get lost down here?" Saja whimpered through chattering teeth.

"I could always dig us out," Smauteken chimed in. "That's what worms are good at—eating mostly but burrowing in the sand is a close second."

Sterling shrugged his shoulders and Green sniffled. The mineral scent of natural rock and stone was foreign but oddly refreshing.

Soon, they rounded a corner, and a pale blue light crept toward them. It grew brighter until the tunnel opened into a vast underground city of structures carved intricately into deep orange and red stone.

Streaks of white and blue liquid flowed down the city's walls, glowing brightly and offering plenty of light to see. Towers of all sizes bore markings in fluorescent paint that glowed bold and beautiful in the light, then breathtakingly luminous in the shadows. Three of the tallest towers were connected by a circular bridge with wide arched windows. The entire city was adorned with hanging spheres filled with glow flies and candle moths—hints of flashing, popping light sparked around each corner. And pale-barked trees, smooth and grand in size, soared the height of the underground cavern. If the top of the city had been bewitched to look like the sky, no one below would be the wiser of their underground whereabouts. It was magnificent.

"The hidden city of Terra, behold!" the potion wizard said.

Everyone stumbled around in awe of the stunning city—so much so that for a moment, no one noticed the potion wizard disappear.

## CHAPTER TWENTY-SIX
# WIZARD'S SPEAK

"Terra is...beautiful," Green announced. His tail peeked from around his body and tilted up and down at the glowing insects darting and whizzing through the air.

"Yes. Maybe too beautiful," Saja said, as flecks of purple ink sputtered onto the stone floor. "I feel like I'm in a dream and cannot wake. I don't like it."

"It's no dream. But I can tell you this place is abandoned," Sterling said. "Look around. No living creatures—except for these glow-in-the-dark bugs. Whatever lived here isn't here now."

"Why did they leave?" Smauteken asked, nervously tapping his front four legs against each other.

Sterling crouched near the tallest tower and studied the markings on the wall. His hunter's instincts perked up, and he noted that the potion wizard was gone. He didn't want to alarm the others, so he decided to distract them until the wizard returned.

"Let's investigate. Can any of you make out this language?" Sterling wiped rust-colored sand from an etching. "It looks like a person with a dagger...and some kind of blob?"

"The blob is nothing I recognize. But that other one's a hunter. He looks like you, Sterling Fierce! I guess all you hunters look alike," Saja said, her wings flashing a purple glow.

"I suppose it does look a little like me. Strange." Sterling sighed. "I wonder what that other marking is?"

Smauteken slinked toward them and turned his worm head side to side, staring at the ancient markings. "I'm not the smartest worm, but I have read (and eaten) a lot of Jeanno's magic history books. Um—that looks an awful lot like the symbol for a witch."

Green barreled over, and his tail bumped into Smauteken. "Oof—sorry, it's got a mind of its own. But this is definitely a witch symbol—a light witch, though. I knew they existed even though my parents swore they didn't—but I knew it!"

A light witch. Sterling's mind drifted into a vision of a pale girl with gleaming eyes of ice-blue surrounded by snow.

"Sterling's frightened of an old drawing—he's as pale as a ghost!" Saja giggled.

Just then, the potion wizard returned with a palmful of sand whirling inside a clear satchel. He had the sacred sand ingredient dandling in his grasp and ducked his head as if he had been followed.

Sterling pushed visions of the light witch to the back of his mind.

"I hope everyone enjoyed their brief stay in the hidden city. Best we take our leave before we become hidden as well," he whispered.

"Hidden?" Green gasped as his tail spun him around and pointed at the city towers melting away.

An invisible goo dripped over the beautiful trees, foot by foot, and it spilled onto the cave floor.

"It's coming toward us, Thahn! Get us out of here!" Sterling hollered, recalling a story about an underground city that swallowed its guests whole. He locked eyes with Green to warn him of the grave danger they were in.

Muttering a spell in wizard language, Thahn hurled everyone through a vertical tunnel leading up to the desert surface but not before a corner of Sterling's cape was eaten by Terra's curse. They burst into the midst of the sand war: puffs of smoke, angry battling spiders, and hooded figures.

"We're blocked in!" Sterling shouted. "We can't get to the skies, we'll be slain out here—even if just by accident."

The potion wizard cast a hazy protection bubble over them, but it was thin and wouldn't hold for long. "Saja, can you clear the smoke with your bubble trick? We just need a small hole to see out," the potion wizard asked.

Saja nodded, fluttering her wings into a perfect purple bubble. She darted into the battle smoke and burrowed through the brown haze.

"I can't...the sand and smoke...can't see." Saja choked out her words from above.

Green's crystal tail lit up, and he zoomed toward Saja, following the tiny opening her bubble had made. He peeked through the gap and spied an odd-shaped cloud in the distance, an image only a dragon would recognize.

"Follow me—I know the way out," Green said, suddenly sounding like a grown-up dragon.

"Green, you're the greatest dragon I know!" Sterling applauded as he climbed onto the scaly back. "Hope you don't mind, but I need a ride."

"I've got you, brother. Just hold on tight!" Green exclaimed. His tail wrapped around the witch hunter's waist like a scaly belt.

"Um, guys?" Smauteken pointed to a path of footprints leading into the hidden city.

"Centipars. They've found us," Barath roared, peering out from the potion wizard's robe.

"Yes, and never a jolly time to encounter them. Upward we go—quickly!" The potion wizard waved his wand frantically.

And they all surged up into the clouds, following the Story Dragon's lead.

"You did well, Green and Saja," the potion wizard remarked. "Rest your minds—allow your energy to restore. Here, I'll secure us together with wizard's twine so we'll stay together while in flight." A zap of blue electric rope floated around everyone. Soon, the ink fly and the Story Dragon dozed off. Smauteken snored from below.

Sterling was tempted to sleep, too, but something nagged at him.

*This isn't the way back to the cave.* Those words repeated in Sterling's mind. He didn't want to panic the others, especially not the young dragon whose scaly back he clung to, as they flew over foreign parts of Everen.

The potion wizard tilted his head to lock eyes with the young hunter.

*No. But it is the way we shall go, Sterling.* His words were clear, though no one else must've heard them because they didn't so much as stir.

*How are you doing that?* Sterling thought.

The potion wizard flashed a grin and sped ahead.

Sterling realized this was wizard speak, a way to communicate with magical beings without anyone overhearing. It was popular among wizards, witches, and likely a dozen other magical creatures, according to his father's library books.

*We aren't going back to the cave.* Sterling realized. *You hid your cauldron because you knew the centipars would find it there. You knew when Smauteken and Saja arrived, you were being tracked.* Sterling said in wizard speak, getting the hang of it despite the dull headache it caused him.

*Ah yes, very clever, my young hunter. Only they weren't tracking me.*

Sterling frowned. *The Story Dragon. His magic's more powerful now—he's easier to find. Right?*

The potion wizard nodded solemnly.

*I'm sorry about your wizard's kitchen—that you had to leave it behind.*

*Oh, don't worry about that, young hunter. They're just things. What matters is that you and Green are safe—and our new friends too.*

# CHAPTER TWENTY-SEVEN

# THE ICE MOUNTAINS

The pack of friends flew until nightfall. In the darkness, the terrain transformed into a mountain range sprinkled with snowy peaks glittering in the moonlight. Clouds jiggled with ice particles, ready to burst open a prickly downpour at any moment. Without warning, the wizard plunged into the heart of the mountains.

"Wake up, sleepyheads! Welcome to the great Ice Mountains," the potion wizard said as the blue electric rope that held them together evaporated into specks of dust. He motioned for them to follow as he glided through dark crevices between giant frozen rocks.

Only a few gray ravens took notice of their presence, casually glancing over with tiny mirrors for eyes. Their black tail feathers twitched in silence. Smauteken and Saja landed inside the mountain on a wide, flat clearing covered with piles of small rocks.

Green, with Sterling on his back, followed. The potion wizard spiraled upward, returning with a frost-covered cauldron and a tall glass phial halfway full of dark liquid and oil bubbles.

"And now, for the sandstone potion," he said calmly, tending to the cauldron. "Any miscalculation and my delicate brew will spoil like poisoned fruit."

While he got to work unraveling and unpacking ingredients from his robe pockets, one of the larger gray ravens flew to the potion wizard's shoulder. The raven's beak opened. She spoke an unfamiliar tongue, certainly not ordinary bird chatter, and nothing close to human, Elvish, or even ancient wizard language.

"I've no time for any disruptions—this potion is the only thing that matters now. If I cannot focus, our quest is doomed," the potion wizard whispered loud enough for Sterling to hear but no one else.

Saja listened keenly. "The raven said something about...no, that can't be right. Footprints?!" the ink fly said under her breath.

Smauteken had started snacking on bits of mountain dust. "Oh yeah, I saw some in the snow when we landed. That's probably what she's talking about."

Saja seethed. "You should have said something, you plumpy-brained worm!"

Smauteken cringed and shut his eyes. After a moment, when no one had thrown anything at him, he peeked out from under his hair. Sterling felt a tinge of heat beneath his skin. Smauteken wasn't very clever, but the worm didn't deserve to live feeling so afraid.

"It's not your fault, Smauteken. But this could be dangerous for all of us. Could you draw the prints to show me what they look like?" Sterling asked as calmly as he could despite the bullets of sweat forming on the back of his neck.

"I suppose so. Um. Worms have excellent memory —sometimes." The hairy worm fiddled about, apparently looking for something to write with. Some of his feet tapped against the mountain floor in rapid clicks.

"Here," said Green as he effortlessly conjured a drawing stick with his magic.

Smauteken drew the prints as precisely as if they were in front of his eyes.

"I recognize them," Sterling said. "Green and Saja, search for any signs of centipars outside the mountain—from the air. See which direction the tracks go. Start at the base of this mountain and circle out from there. But don't let them see you. Use whatever camouflage you have but remember centipars can smell magic. Smauteken, don't take your eyes off the mountain's entrance." Sterling sounded like his father giving directions before a hunt. "The potion wizard needs time to finish the sandstone. I'll stand guard."

*Thank you,* the potion wizard said to Sterling in wizard speak. He didn't look up from his potion. Instead, ingredients darted through the air and tumbled into the brew at high speed, as precise as always.

The cave was eerily quiet after Green and Saja departed, but the cauldron's bubbling soon calmed Sterling. In all the commotion, Barath had hidden away in his bark—likely upset about the cold temperature that even the mountain walls could not shut out. Sterling missed his banter and his wisdom, as grumpy as it was.

Soon, the sixth stone of the seven sisters appeared, the Sandstone of Time glowing a golden brown, twinkling with inner flames. The seven sisters spoke. They sounded strong and somehow younger than before. Sterling felt the heat from the stone in his core—it pulsed, more potent than the first five.

"Must you?" complained Barath, his wooden eyelids finally opening. "Are you going to shine that light in my eyes until they turn to ash?"

"Oh, look who decided to grace us with his consciousness! We're nearing the end of our adventure after all," the potion wizard said. He tapped his wand across Barath's trunk, and the meute's bark shifted, revealing a hidden knothole. It closed around the sandstone.

"Not another one," Barath moaned.

"Yes, yes. Safest place for now. Ah! Before we move on to the last bit, here's a small token to say thank you." The potion wizard hummed as he braided strands of light with his wand, pushing them toward Barath in a magical glow.

Barath's wilted palm leaves crumpled onto the rocky floor before hustling away with the next arctic gust. Deep green prickles sprouted across Barath until he resembled a tiny evergreen tree.

"I could use pinecones while you're at it." Barath sneezed. "Brr." He shook ice droplets from his branches toward the potion wizard.

"Yes, go ahead and shake your branches. You're a real pine tree now!" The potion wizard dabbed away a glittery bead of sweat from his brow. "Back to work—the last recipe is a doozy!"

But before the potion wizard could gather the ingredient list for the seventh and final stone, a commotion stirred.

"Something's coming!" Smauteken hollered.

"Centipars! They're here!" Green bellowed as he tumbled inside the mountain's lair, one ripped wing flapping in the arctic wind.

Sterling used his hunter's vision, which revealed the Story Dragon's belly was covered in claw marks and splashed with purple ink. Saja was nowhere in sight.

# CHAPTER TWENTY-EIGHT

# A BATTLE INSIDE THE MOUNTAIN

"Go! Hide deep in the mountain," shouted Sterling, unsheathing the silvery-blue dagger from his waist. "I'll fight them."

Saja appeared as if out of thin air, hovering above Sterling's shoulder. Her antennae and some round blobs on her body perked up, filling with purple ink. It would've been nonthreatening, except some plum-colored juice sputtered out and burned steaming holes into the mountain rock wall behind her.

"We'll fight them together," she said.

"Where were you?" Smauteken whined.

"I applied some slippery obstacles for our company—it won't stop them, but it will slow them down," Saja said with a wink.

Green's eyes flashed a bright amber, and his crystal tail pulsed a bright, clear white. "I will fight too." He closed his eyes, and a thin skin of crystal grew over his whole body, bandaging his cuts and patching up the damage in his wing.

Smauteken wiggled his worm whiskers and scurried out of sight, muttering something about "doing some worm thinking underground...how worms think best."

Sterling locked eyes with the potion wizard. "Go somewhere safe—you have one last potion to brew. We'll hold them off as long as we can."

*Take care of your brave friends and yourself.* He wizard-speak-whispered as he and his frosty cauldron vanished in a puff of smoke.

Sterling, Green, and Saja prepared to battle the centipars, taking cover behind a pair of boulders. The potion wizard concealed himself on a high ledge, Barath at his side, to conjure the final stone. Sparks of magic swarmed around him, searching for the final ingredient.

Without warning, Sterling's mind attuned to the potion wizard's thoughts, and his vision split. Behind the boulder with Green and Saja, he could see from his right eye. From his left came a hazy image and voices in his ear.

"The final stone—this is it. We've almost made it," the potion wizard said.

"It's lucky for you another cauldron was here," Barath pointed out.

"There's no such thing as luck, Barath. You know that!" the potion wizard scolded. "There are other potion wizards out there—I had arranged—oh, don't worry your ancient tree brains about it. The point is, we have what we need." He cast a protection spell over his friends below (Everen knows how long it'll hold), and he got to work on his potion.

"And how do you suppose we'll get that Ice Dragon scale—the most important ingredient for your last stone brew?" Barath inquired.

"I haven't time for our bickering routine now. The winged snow beasts are nearly here. They'll be after blood this time," the potion wizard warned.

Barath instinctively touched his trunk scars.

Mountain rock plopped into the brew along with raven talons and blood droppings from arctic spiders. Blue fire crept over the edges of the cauldron. Black oil bubbles rumbled in the mix, growing larger and bursting with a grotesque smacking sound. Shiny black goo stained the rocky ledge.

"We're ready for the Ice Dragon scale. It's here, hidden within the mountain crevices, wishing not to be found—not by me, anyway. The Story Dragon is the key, as the sisters said! It's as plain as the whiskers in my beard!"

"What in Everen are you talking about?" Barath hissed.

Just then, a heavy presence approached the mountain. Sterling's head pounded like he'd thumped it on a metal box.

"I hear them. Big flapping wings!" Green whispered.

Four long-feathered centipars landed inside the

mountain, claws clacking against the cold mountain rock.

"Their eyes! Look—purple splatter in a shade I recognize," Sterling said in a hushed voice. "Saja, you did well."

"The ink's temporary, but at least we can get a good look at them before they come at us," Saja explained.

But the centipars sniffed the air.

"They're tracking us," Sterling said knowingly. "Brace yourselves!"

Predatory eyes darted toward the magical trio, and the centipars charged in a flurry of talons and beaks as black as night.

*Smack!* The largest one crashed into the wizard's protection shield with claws at the ready. The shield blinked a pale white and repaired its punctured spots like clear wax being reformed.

"The protection shield is holding!" Green said with a naïve smile.

*Smack! Smack! Smack!* The centipars, one after the other, took turns barreling into the shield. Each time, it took longer to reform; it subtly grew thinner.

"I don't know how much longer it'll hold. Saja, Green, be ready; let them use their energy to come at you. Don't go to them first," Sterling instructed, clenching his dagger.

Green's tail tapped the dragon's shoulder and pointed. When he looked up, all four centipars locked wings and formed into one giant, feathery boulder that barreled straight at them.

# CHAPTER TWENTY-NINE

# THE DARK WIZARDS

I n a loud crash, the protection shield shattered. It dissolved into flurrying magic particles. A huge centipar, adorned with shiny black eyes and scarred fur on its stomach, leaped onto Barath (no one had seen the tiny meute make his way down from the ledge).

"No!" Sterling screamed, racing toward the black-eyed beast.

He aimed his blade at its throat.

The beast scratched deep into the trunk's core. Barath shot pine needles into his attacker's face then hid in his bark. Again, the centipar readied its talons.

Wings fluttered past its nose, teasing its feline instincts (it was half big cat, after all). It abandoned the log and sprinted toward Saja. It never saw the witch hunter spring from atop a boulder until he had slammed onto its back, driving his knife deep. Sterling's dagger slipped as he clung to blood-slick feathers. The centipar bellowed in pain and sank to the ground. Sterling drew back his dagger to make sure the beast stayed down, but there was a faint gasp, and he whirled to Saja.

A second beast had plucked the ink fly out of the air, its jaws sunk into her body. She squirmed feebly as catlike claws battered her. Bits of beautiful shimmering wings whirled in the cold air.

Purple lights flashed, then went black.

Sterling felt a cold lump in his throat like he was swallowing blocks of ice.

"Sterling Fierce! Help!" the Story Dragon called.

He turned and sprinted toward Green. The pack leader, the largest centipar, must have known that Green was too powerful to be defeated in a fair fight. Instead, it distracted the dragon by flitting around, pecking at him. Green's crystal armor was flaking off all over his body, and he panted through a rivulet of blood from a deep gash on his forehead. He dodged backward—right into a trap.

"Green! Watch out!" Sterling hollered.

But it was too late. A boulder tipped over the mountain's ledge and came down at a speed sure to smash him into dragon bits. The hidden centipar peered over the ledge, cackled, and flew right at Sterling.

He readied his dagger, still stained with tar-like centipar blood, and thrust it into the sharp black feathers as the creature pounced.

*Ka-Boom!*

In the smoky explosion, Sterling lost sight of everything. His chest and arms were covered in something sticky—centipar blood and possibly his own.

Two glassy black eyes appeared, staring blankly into his own. Instinctively, Sterling pressed his dagger against the centipar's throat. The monster was warm but without a heartbeat, the telltale signs of a hunter's success.

With the strength he had left, he searched the smoke for his dragon friend.

"Green! Are you alright?"

In the silence, three security bubbles rose above the smoke. Each one contained a centipar: the pack leader, Saja's attacker, and an injured one oozing black goo (courtesy of the hunter's dagger). They snarled and clawed in frustration, but they were trapped. Having blasted his way into the battle, the potion wizard dispensed some magical justice—and just in time.

"Thahn! Thahn saved us!" Green cried out, bouncing toward the potion wizard.

"For now. But Green, you must save us all. You must fly high into the mountain and find the ice scale. It is hidden from me—from everyone but you. Only a Story Dragon can find it—it will call to you. Now go! Fly!" the potion wizard explained.

Green covered himself in magic crystal once again and took flight, spiraling into the blackness of rocky passageways, listening for a call, but nothing came to him. He flew, searched, and scanned every ledge and crevice of the mountain.

"It's no use. I'm a mistake—I'm not a real Story Dragon," Green sobbed. But, then, a familiar feeling came over him, like his parents' embrace. It called to him. His tears dried up as he swooped toward a glimmer in the rocks.

Once Green had the ice scale in his grasp, he dove back down the mountain. The potion wizard slipped it into the cauldron. But nothing happened.

Clawing and growling vibrated from the centipars in their temporary security bubbles.

"What's wrong?" Green asked. "It's not working— the spell—the potion. Did I get the wrong scale?"

"Hold still, buddy." Sterling had begun bandaging the dragon's wounds with torn-off pieces of his hunter's cape. He had rushed to Barath and Saja, but there wasn't much he could do for either. Barath had retreated into his bark, and Saja didn't respond either. He blinked back tears and tried to concentrate.

*Dragon blood is stubborn. It keeps soaking through,* Sterling said in wizard speak.

The potion wizard paced back and forth as the ice scale surfaced in his silvery brew and made a gurgling sound. *Patience, my young hunter. This is the best part,* the wizard spoke back.

Green stopped wiggling and his eyes shone bright emerald as they locked on to the scale. "I know what I'm supposed to do," he said, before he plucked the ice scale out of the brew with his tail and secured it on his back. He scooped up Barath and zoomed to the top of the mountain faster than he'd ever flown before.

The mountain shook, and frozen bits of rock rained down, pelting them both.

"What in Everen?" Sterling jumped in front of the wizard and his cauldron.

A crowd of beings floated into the mountain, long dark robes wisping across the cold floor. Three more packs of centipars had arrived. They split up and circled Sterling and the potion wizard.

"It's the Ottomon clan," the potion wizard whispered. The worry in his voice was unmistakable, and Sterling's stomach knotted up.

Jeanno the Twisted was cloaked in a blackish-green robe that trailed behind him at least the length of his tall, lean body. His one natural eye glowed a mystical emerald, and he clasped a bicolored wand forged from wrangled root—a species that only grew in the depths of the dark forest's remains. Sterling could sense that it was enchanted with dark magic and, like its master, the roots were twisted.

"Such a peculiar choice for a hiding place. Though, a frigid mountain that was once home to the cowardly ice wizards does compliment the betrayal of your kind, Thahn. Such a waste of talent to try to save those worthless, power-hungry dragons. *Tsk, tsk.* You could've been so much more." Jeanno's nasal voice echoed loudly in the mountain halls.

"You are wrong about the dragons, Jeanno, and

you are wrong about a great many other things," the potion wizard said with might.

"I haven't time for your foolishness. I banish you from the wizardly world, Thahn of Edmonstone, for your treachery against wizards. There shall be no friends of dragons among us." Jeanno twitched his wand, sending a flurry of centipars toward the potion wizard, who had no choice but to release his hold on the security bubbles, instantly releasing the agitated centipars. He flung up a shield around himself and the young witch hunter beside him.

All the beasts were free to attack them. Two packs of Cultid centipars sprang at Sterling, yellow pointed teeth bared. Falcut centipars soared above them, diving one by one to pick at the potion wizard. Blue Herikats tracked the scent they craved, spiraling to the top of the mountain after the prized Story Dragon.

# CHAPTER THIRTY

# THE TRUTH OF THE STORY DRAGON

Centipars flew, sprang, and sprinted straight for the potion wizard's collapsing shields. The pack leader hurled its muscular 600-pound half-cat, half-bird body at Sterling.

*I wish I didn't know the details,* he thought as he was knocked flat on his back. His dagger glowed an Elvish blue amid a fury of midnight feathers and razor-sharp talons. Simultaneously, a Blue Herikat dove to rip apart the potion wizard, fangs at the ready. The wizard's troll-teeth staff beamed with pure white light, and the mountain shook violently.

"Go forth! All creatures—you dine on magical blood tonight!" Jeanno said as he waved more than a dozen centipars forward, urging their primal instincts to reign and destroy his foe.

"And what of the human?" A beast snarled at Jeanno.

"Kill the boy too!" he snapped.

Amid the assault of inevitable slaughter, a massive gooey head burst from the mountain's center. It towered above them—a giant mountain worm, legendary and not seen since the time of the ancients. Her eyes were enormous, pale white, and filled with hunger like a colossal Smauteken ready to devour an entire village of books.

"Smauteken!" Sterling screamed, pointing at the tiny worm riding on top of the monstrous rock giant.

Smauteken smiled, then shut his eyes and clung to the mountain worm's back. The giant worm sucked in a breath and darted forward, snatching the entire pack of Blue Herikats and gobbling them down. Then she swallowed both packs of Cultid. One after the other, muscular furry bodies and wings disappeared past her blue-stained lips. The Falcut retreated, along with Sterling's attacker, the pack leader, flying at top speed (they were the wisest of the centipars). The Ottomon Wizards raised their wands and sent a huge wave of sizzling light at the giant worm, but the spell fizzled. Sterling stared wide-eyed at the plumb-colored splatters that seemed to appear from nowhere. Wizards shrieked as acid began searing skin and clothes, and they were suddenly gone, deserting Jeanno to fight his own war.

Saja dropped her camouflage and came to a stop at Sterling's feet, her body pulsing faintly. As fast as she'd appeared, the giant rock worm descended back down into the mountain's depths, and Smauteken plopped down next to Saja, propping her up with three of his soft, furry feet.

Unfazed, Jeanno jabbed his gnarled wand in the potion wizard's direction.

"It doesn't matter what friends you've made. My power is all I need to destroy you. The dragons will never return!" Jeanno shouted, shooting glowing purple flames and bursts of light at Thahn.

*Hunter, I've no energy left. I need your help!* The potion wizard pleaded.

Sterling's mind burst with images of witches he'd fought, and his hunter's blood boiled. From his forearms, he shot a bloodred shield into Thahn's grip as he jumped in front of Smauteken and Saja to block them from the explosion. Bolts of burning light bounced off the shield. It caught fire and burned violently, forming a whirlwind of black-and-purple flames that stretched outward like evil, spindly fingers. They grasped for the potion wizard and slapped the shield out of his hands. As fiery fingers clutched Thahn, the witch hunter leaped from above, slicing the flamed digits off with a glistening red sword.

Jeanno squealed, "No! A blood sword! What are you—who are you, boy!?"

As the flickering hand retreated, a stray fiery bolt hammered across Smauteken's round, hairy bottom, caught in the crossfire.

"Yeow!" cried Smauteken.

"He's hurt badly!" the potion wizard thundered as he dropped to the ground next to the injured worm.

The worm's gash oozed with poison. Sterling could smell it.

"Another weak soul. A traitor! A dimwit with hair instead of brains," Jeanno seethed. "This insolent worm summoned this beast—she's eaten my loyal centipars. You will die for this, Smauteken. You and your friends will pay with your meaningless lives!"

Jeanno targeted his most potent shot, a flying mirrored blade known as the Face of Death, directly at Smauteken.

A bloodstone emerged from Sterling's veins, and he took aim. The Face of Death left Jeanno's hand, bumped ever so slightly by the tiny red stone. Death's dagger cut through the air toward Smauteken and the depleted potion wizard kneeling beside him.

It punctured the potion wizard's cap.

"A hunter's aim!" Jeanno squealed. "No matter—I have one more shot of magic left, and I assure you it's a fatal blow!" Jeanno pointed the end of his staff at Smauteken, and it began to sputter black tar and smoke.

A blast like a cannon boomed inside the mountain as Jeanno's attack discharged.

But at that moment, a bubble of sea-green-tinted crystal wrapped around Smauteken. Another appeared around Saja, then the largest surrounded Thahn and Sterling.

"What in all of Everen's stars?" Sterling whispered.

"Okay, now it's the best part—took longer than I expected, but you can't rush miracles, now, can you, Sterling Fierce?" Thahn said, with a knowing grin.

A huge green dragon with brilliant emerald eyes swooped down with cold mountain air. Flames went out, and even Jeanno stared in awe. It was the Story Dragon, evolved into his true, powerful form, adorned with seven glowing scales atop his back, each the color of the seven sisters' stones.

Bearing the sisters' ancient gifts, Green conjured Mountain Breath and blew Jeanno into frozen rock before hurling him far away into the icy sky. Activating the Forest Stone of Life's power, Green pulled the dark wizard's poison from Smauteken's body. It dried into a smooth bluish scar, and Smauteken opened his eyes. Green set Barath on the stone floor. The Healing Stone of the Sea's power glowed from another dragon scale, beaming light onto the meute's trunk, mending his deep wound but leaving a telltale imperfection. Finally, Green used the Sky Stone of Mobility's power to repair Saja's ripped wing and leaking ink, waking her from a painful sleep. Her new wing was a luminous shade of sea green—stronger than ever.

Last, a zap from a crimson scale, the Fire Stone of Energy's magic replenished the potion wizard's strength, and a flicker of red fire struck Sterling's dagger, causing it to blaze reddish flames from its edges. The Story Dragon winked. *That's for you, my brother.*

"We've done it! Green, my Story Dragon, the seven sisters live again. Their power lives within YOU!" The potion wizard smiled. The tip of his wand glowed with fire magic.

Spiraling high into the mountaintop, Green sent spells from the Sandstone of Time and the Ice Stone of Wisdom in a flurry of spherical shapes, twisting and writing with bright colors and electric fireworks. When all settled, the smell of burnt energy and cold smoke filled the mountain.

The seven sisters sang, their voices filling the mountain's innards:

*"In times of darkness and greed,*
*There will be born a Story Dragon, a special breed,*
*To secure good magic and save his kind,*
*No purer spirit in Everen, you'll find.*
*Our magic lives in his scales,*
*The seven sisters and the Story Dragon, faithful in all the*
*tales."*

Out of the corners of the mountain, baby Ice Dragons emerged.

"They have been reborn. All the dragons," Green explained in a deep voice.

The potion wizard wiped his brow. "Yes, one by one, dragons will return to the land, the sea, the sky, and the mountains—to all of Everen. Once again, there are dragons, and as long as our Story Dragon is here, there always will be."

With all right again in the magic realm, Sterling returned home and brought Smauteken and Saja to live with his Uncle Roag (they fit right in with the rest of the odd creatures he kept). Green and the potion wizard carried on with plans to build a dragon fortress, to the dismay and grumbling of Barath.

Sterling sat in the Alin's library one evening, a thick encyclopedia of magical creatures open on his lap.

"I'll never have my father back, but I do have a family," he said. He turned to Tomorak. "Did you know?"

The Alin smiled faintly.

Sterling turned back to the window and his sharp hunter's eyes caught a glimpse of the Story Dragon's glowing green tail riding through the clouds. And he knew it was only a matter of time before he'd be summoned for another quest—another magical adventure. He could feel it in his blood.

# A LOOK AT BOOK TWO:
## STERLING FIERCE AND THE LIGHT WITCH

**Join Sterling on a daring quest to locate the village elder's granddaughter, a rare light witch.**

Sterling Fierce, the last witch hunter in Bren Village—of the lands of Everen—is on a daring quest to locate the village elder's granddaughter, who just happens to be a rare light witch. Sending a witch hunter to rescue his natural adversary is fraught with risk, but it's Bren's sole hope for continued safety.

Locked away by her elders in isolation, Evenna's magic will certainly go dark—and then Sterling's own powers would certainly destroy her. Together, they embark on a journey filled with conflicting magical forces, challenging the very nature of the relationship between witches and witch hunters. And if the rumors of an impending elvish war are true, forming an unlikely alliance becomes their only path to make it through Everen's wilds and survive the looming conflict.

With centuries of magical bloodlines, what happens when a new generation strives to rewrite their destiny?

*AVAILABLE MARCH 2024*

# ACKNOWLEDGMENTS

I have many debts that I owe each editor, writer, and reader with whom I have had the extreme fortune of crossing paths over the years. In particular, Sirah Jarocki has been on this journey with me at each step, graciously dusting my stories with her editing magic.

I want to express my extreme gratitude to Wise Wolf Books for their support and David Beers, my mentor, a talented author, and friend. A special tip of the wizard's cap to Stephanie Giambattista for her encouragement and for sharing my stories with her class.

My husband, James, and my sons, Brenner and Bryce, tolerated many nights and weekends with me tucked away in my writing corner. I could not have done this without their love, patience, and support.

Lastly, I want to say thank you to my mom, Pamela, and my sister, Julie, for always being there for me.

# ABOUT THE AUTHOR

Lori Tchen was born and raised in the Texas hill country where shaking out one's shoes for scorpions was part of the daily norm. She writes fiction in the evenings, her highly prized downtime outside of work, while raising her two sons.

Lori's career began in criminology, working deep nights in a detention facility, then investigating crimes as a Texas State Enforcement Agent. After observing the underbelly of society, her fantasy stories allow her and her readers to escape into imagined worlds and inspire bravery in children (and adults alike) to face some of life's evil characters.

www.ingramcontent.com/pod-product-compliance
Lightning Source LLC
Chambersburg PA
CBHW011435240626
47153CB00011B/3004